Israel

By
Avery Gale

The Adlers

The siblings. Their occupations and ages at the beginning of the series:

Austin – 31 – CEO of the family oil conglomerate based in Austin, TX. Married to magical, Charlotte.

Asia – 30 – Ruthless legal eagle for the family business. Married to Franklin Cordesi.

Bronx – 29 – Owns a string of car dealerships in partnership with brother, Cleveland.

Cleveland – 28 – Race car driver. Astral traveler. Married to Vienna Quan.

Brooklyn – 27 – Retrieval expert for big insurance companies. Semi-retired in subsequent books. Security consultant. Married to Luke Grayson, lives in New Mexico. Daughter, Crystal.

Catalina – 26 – Freelance intelligent agent working with the CIA, MI6, Mossad, and others. Travels the world as a successful jewelry designer.

Israel – 25 – Security expert and tracker.

Kensington – 24 – Actor. Married to Denali West.

London – 23 – Chemist/Researcher. Married to shifters, Elijah & Evan Monroe. They live outside Boston and have twin sons.

Paris – 22 – Recent College Graduate. Mated with Sheriff Trinity Stone. School Administrator and teacher.

Watch this page for updates in subsequent books in this series.

The Adlers

The siblings. Their occupations and ages at the beginning of the series:

Austin – 31 – CEO of the family oil conglomerate based in Austin, TX. Married to magical, Charlotte.

Asia – 30 – Ruthless legal eagle for the family business. Married to Franklin Cordesi.

Bronx – 29 – Owns a string of car dealerships in partnership with brother, Cleveland.

Cleveland – 28 – Race car driver. Astral traveler. Married to Vienna Quan.

Brooklyn – 27 – Retrieval expert for big insurance companies. Semi-retired in subsequent books. Security consultant. Married to Luke Grayson, lives in New Mexico. Daughter, Crystal.

Catalina – 26 – Freelance intelligent agent working with the CIA, MI6, Mossad, and others. Travels the world as a successful jewelry designer.

Israel – 25 – Security expert and tracker.

Kensington – 24 – Actor. Married to Denali West.

London – 23 – Chemist/Researcher. Married to shifters, Elijah & Evan Monroe. They live outside Boston and have twin sons.

Paris – 22 – Recent College Graduate. Mated with Sheriff Trinity Stone. School Administrator and teacher.

Watch this page for updates in subsequent books in this series.

Chapter One

I T'S HER.

    She's here.

Finally.

Israel couldn't believe he'd finally found his mate. Well, found wasn't entirely accurate, but she was nearby. That had to count for something. Watching his younger siblings find their mates was past the point of discouraging. If you'd asked him two years ago, he'd have said he didn't plan to settle down before he was thirty, but with his brothers and sisters finding their mates, finding his own seemed more and more appealing. And to be honest, he was pushing closer to the age milestone than he wanted to admit.

"Did you say something? What's wrong?" As the oldest of ten, Austin Adler was usually tuned in to his younger brothers and sisters, and today was no exception. Even though Israel hadn't said anything out loud, it wasn't a surprise his brother heard him. As shifters, they communicated telepathically, and the habit often slipped into their everyday lives without any of them taking notice.

"My mate. She's here. I don't know where, but she's close." Turning his head in an attempt to follow the scent,

Israel zeroed in on a nearby group of women who were busy setting out enough food to feed an army. The invitation to Kensington and Denali's wedding had been limited to a select group of family and friends, but the reception was going to be much larger.

"At the rate people are streaming into this place, you'd better get a move on before she gets lost in the damned crowd. I need to head out, anyway. I want to find my own lovely mate, and she'd better be sitting down with her feet up, or it's not going to go well for her. Did you know babies could get their days and nights confused? How does that happen when they are supposed to sleep all the damned time? Holy hell, you won't believe the paraphernalia they require, and if our sisters don't stop sending Charlotte *'you must have this gadget'* suggestions, I'm going to go postal."

Israel was only half-listening to his brother's crazed ranting. With a rapidly growing number of nieces and nephews, he'd learned new parents tended to occasionally tip over the edge of sanity. He didn't have any children of his own, so it was a mystery to Israel why they all seemed to think he could help, so he usually turned a deaf ear to the chatter. He planned to play the hell out of the *uncle card* once the kiddos were old enough to spoil properly, without any remote chance, he'd be roped into anything involving diapers.

"Who is the woman on the right?" Israel didn't take his eyes off her. He wasn't close enough to confirm she was *his one*, but there was something about her...

"The blonde? Dr. Bristol Banks. She is Charlotte's obstetrician. Well, not just hers, she's the OB for our pack and many of the club members as well." Knowing she was the preferred doctor for those two groups told Israel a lot, but not enough. "I'm surprised you didn't scent her when you took Charlotte for her appointment."

Early in her pregnancy, Israel intercepted Austin's wayward wife when she'd tried to sneak out of the building without an escort. Unfortunately for Charlotte, when any of the Adlers were in danger or experiencing a health crisis, they were immediately subject to extra security protections. By the time Israel was alerted the little minx had left the penthouse, she was already in the elevator on her way to the garage. He'd had to hustle but managed to be waiting for her.

"Are you kidding? I didn't go in with her. I escorted her to the door and waited in my car. Way too much estrogen in there for me—although in hindsight, that might have been a bad call." Without waiting for Austin to respond, Israel started across the slate-lined pavilion between the small Forum Shops. He saw the moment she realized he was headed her way—her body stiffened, her bright blue eyes going impossibly wide.

Oh, fuck me six ways to... No. No. Just frick-fracking, No. I don't have time for this shit.

Well, well. It doesn't seem my fated mate is thrilled with my appearance. Interesting. The wind was in his favor, the breeze bringing her tantalizing scent to him in fragrant waves of temptation, but it hadn't kept her from recognizing him. In the few seconds it took him to close the distance between them, Israel realized two things. First, Bristol Banks was his mate. Second, she was not pleased. Whether it was him personally or being mated in general, remained to be seen.

DR. BRISTOL BANKS was enjoying the break in her regular routine. Two years ago, she'd vowed to scale back her workload, fearing fate would saddle her with a mate before she'd had enough time to enjoy the life she'd worked so hard to establish. It took her over a year to find a physician she felt confident bringing into her specialized practice.

With fewer medical professionals opting for obstetrics and gynecology, due to the astronomical liability insurance costs, the options were limited. Further narrowing the field to a shifter who understood kink made finding a partner almost impossible. It hadn't been easy, but she didn't have a choice. Bristol had been forced to admit, operating the clinic was more than she could handle alone.

Shaking off her concerns about work, Bristol set the doctor side of her life aside. Today was all about having fun and celebrating love. It was particularly wonderful since she wasn't the one who was now tied down to one man for the rest of her life. It wasn't as though Bristol enjoyed a plethora of men and a kick-ass sex life, but if the tide turned, she wanted to be ready.

Since shifters mated for life, Bristol planned to delay mating as long as possible. The extended lifespan of magicals was a mixed blessing, in her opinion. Shit, what if she ended up mated to an asshole? She wouldn't even be able to throw his hairy ass off a bridge... damn that pesky Hippocratic Oath, anyway! Rolling her eyes at the bizarre direction her thoughts had taken, Bristol carried out the last tray of sandwiches from the makeshift kitchen. Laughing with the other club submissives who'd been asked to help with the reception was good for her soul.

"Damn, I'm so excited. I was honored when Master Kyle called. It's always nice to be trusted... I didn't care who was getting married. Nope, it didn't matter because Tobi's parties are always the best." Anna Griffin was practically dancing in place.

"True, but holy freaking hippos on holiday... we got to attend Kensington Adler's wedding reception. That is pretty amazing." Bristol had to agree, Tobi was a ton of fun, but being able to attend a movie star's wedding was beyond cool.

"I'm putting it on my resume. Not the details—hell, just attending a star-studded event is enough to set me apart from the others." They all laughed, but Bristol thought there was a strong possibility the young coed was serious. Lindy Timish was in her final semester of graduate law school and was supposed to take the bar exam in a few months. Everyone was taking bets on whether Cameron Barnes found some way to stop her from moving out.

"You're assuming Master Barnes lets you out of the house to take the bar." Kim Salter, a senior in economics, planned to stay in Austin. The Wests had helped her secure a job with one of the biggest banks in Texas. From what Bristol had seen, Kim was as brilliant as she was beautiful.

"He'll let me out for the test, but I'm not sure he'll let me move out if I pass and find a job anywhere other than Austin—at least until his Chloe and Phillip leave for college." The slender beauty rolled her green eyes and laughed, "I swear CeCe is going to miss me more than the kids. For the most part, I've transitioned to household manager and chauffeur. Let's face it, the kids don't really need a nanny, but adult supervision is a plus anytime Kodi is home."

Bristol met Cameron and Dr. CeCe Barnes at Prairie Winds not long after she moved to Austin, but she'd only recently met their spirited young daughter. Cecelia Barnes was one of the most widely respected pediatric surgeons in the world, and her husband was a retired CIA intelligence officer. According to club gossip, the *retired* part of that description was questionable at best and more likely, a gross exaggeration.

"Who. Is. That? I'm telling you, that man is damned hot." Anna was fanning herself, but Bristol wasn't sure who she was referring to.

"Bronx Adler. It has to be genetics. All the Adler men are good looking. This is the first time I've seen him. His sisters told me he works all the time." Living with the Barnes meant Lindy always knew who was who in the zoo.

"To heck with that. Who wants a man who's all work and no play?"

Bristol understood the young woman's sentiment, but having a man who was driven held a lot of appeal. The men she'd met recently were more interested in their sports cars, boats, and jet skis than they were setting themselves up for the future.

Anna shrugged her shoulders, "I don't know if he's a Dom, but I could probably do vanilla for a few months... maybe."

"Who are you kidding? You wouldn't last a month." Kim was probably right. Anna was a masochist. It was doubtful she would ever be satisfied with vanilla sex.

Bristol shook her head, laughing at the three women she considered friends. After fast-tracking through school, it was often hard to remember these women were all her age.

"Bronx and Israel are the only Adler men who are still single." Anna fanned herself and grinned. "Master Israel is drool-worthy and pure magic with a flogger. He doesn't like to leave marks that will last more than a few hours. I have to negotiate like a wild woman anytime I want to scene with him, but it's worth it."

"I'd never reached subspace before my scene with him. Too bad he's such a commitment-phobe." Kim had obviously understood her scene with the gifted Master Israel was nothing more than mutual play.

Flogger? Subspace? Hell, how had she missed meeting Israel Adler? She'd met various members of his family, but for some reason, their paths had never crossed.

"Don't look now, but he's headed this way." Anna nudged Kim, nodding her head toward a man stalking across the courtyard.

"Damn, he is in full-on Dom mode and lasered in on you, Dr. B." Lindy's warning was unnecessary—the hair on the back of Bristol's neck was already standing on end. She tried to pull in a deep breath but suddenly felt as though all the air had been sucked away from where she stood. The panic of not being able to breathe only lasted a few seconds, but it was long enough to make her heart skip a couple of beats. The combination deprived her brain of enough oxygen for her legs to get the message to run. *Fucking hell, I don't need this.* He was close... much too close by the time she pulled her head out of her ass and turned to retreat. *No. No....*

"Stop." One word, but it was enough for her to freeze. *Shit, shit, shit.* What a lousy time for her naturally submissive nature to surface. A warm hand wrapped around her upper arm, and she felt herself being propelled forward. "Come. We need to talk." The words were spoken softly, the warmth of his breath brushing the shell of her ear, making her shiver as goosebumps raced over the surface of her exposed skin. Of course, she'd chosen today, of all days, to wear her sexiest halter dress. The material of the full skirt floated around her full hips, hiding the curves she could never seem to lose, no matter how much time she spent at the gym. The halter left her back exposed all the way to her waist—it was the sexiest piece of clothing she owned. There wasn't a chance in hell he'd miss her reaction to his touch.

"I wouldn't be a very good Dom if I missed such a telling response to my touch, would I?" Bristol fought the urge to roll her eyes—a move trained submissives knew was a sure ticket to a punishment scene. *Nope, not going to fall into that trap.* "Pity. I think we'd both enjoy your spanking more than you're willing to admit."

Bristol was a shifter and understood telepathic communication, but she was shocked by his ability to tap into her thoughts. She needed to research ways to block the intrusion. *Fuck it, let him figure out this isn't happening. I have no desire to be tied down.*

"Watch your language, Beautiful. This wasn't on my agenda for today, either, but you know what? If I've learned one thing about fate, it's the Universal Force operates on its own timeline. What you or I might have had planned just flew out the window, Sweetheart." He rounded the corner of a tall hedge, turning her so quickly, she stumbled against him.

Damn sky-high heels. She was much more comfortable in the athletic shoes she wore to work. A lot of medical professionals wore clogs, but Bristol had never been able to keep the damned things on while sprinting between patients who always seemed to go into labor at the same time.

The sudden contact of her body pressed against his brought her up short, making her suck in a deep breath. *Mistake. Huge error. Monumental blunder*. Prior to their physical contact, his scent only been teasing her senses—now, it overwhelmed her. For several seconds, Bristol was lost in a fog of desire so strong, she felt herself sway. The haze of lust was a lure, making her worry her knees were going to fold out from under her. Cream flooded her pussy lips in preparation for mating as her labia swelled with blood rushing into the tender tissues. She had a split second to send up a silent prayer, he wouldn't notice her body's autonomic changes, but her hope was dashed when his pupils dilated, and his nostrils flared.

Fucking hell.

Chapter Two

ISRAEL HAD NEVER had a woman respond physically as perfectly as Bristol. Her reaction was especially significant since he sensed she was fighting the attraction with every fiber of her being. He suddenly wished he'd spent more than the few minutes reviewing the background check his company did for Austin when Charlotte chose Dr. Banks as her obstetrician. The only detail he remembered from the security clearance was she'd graduated from every educational level early and was one of the most respected OB/GYNs in the southern half of the country.

Israel's hand spanned the width of her bare back, holding her against his chest after she stumbled into him, the contact sending a surge of blood to his cock. He was pleased when the enticing scent of her arousal surrounded him—nice to know he wasn't the only one affected. The lovely doctor stayed pressed against him for several seconds, the temptation building to the point, he wasn't sure he could hold it back. He wanted nothing more than to pull aside whatever scrap of nothing she was wearing under the loose flowing skirt and plunge himself as deep as her delectable body would allow.

Tucked behind a hedge during his brother and new

sister-in-law's wedding reception was not the time or place to claim his mate, no matter how tempting. Israel didn't try to mask his interest. She had every right to know how much he wanted her. It was damned satisfying to watch her blue eyes widen as the pulse at the base of her throat pounded so fast, he knew she'd begin to feel lightheaded if she didn't rein it in soon. Her breasts pressed against his torso, peaked nipples poking into his chest, the invitation rocketing his desire into the stratosphere. Soon he wouldn't be able to resist taking her—propriety would no longer be enough of a deterrent.

"I want you, Beautiful. Your scent is imprinting itself on my very soul, but you deserve more from me than to be claimed this way." She took a half step back, paused long enough to pull in a deep breath, then moved back another step. She was still close enough to touch, but the small distance between them gave the two of them enough space to catch their breath.

"I don't want this." She dropped her gaze to the ground, sighing in resignation. "Mating, I mean. I won't insult your intelligence by denying I'm physically attracted to you. I don't lie... hell, it wouldn't do any good, anyway. My physiological responses are too obvious to ignore. Damn traitorous hormones." Israel had to bite back his amusement. She awfully cute when she was grumpy. He wondered how often her speech kicked into doctor-mode.

"We'll talk about it later. Where is your phone, Beautiful?" Bristol lifted her gaze to meet his. When she blinked several times, obviously trying to focus on the question rather than her racing heart, he slid his hand around the sexy curve of her bare neck. Using the pads of his fingers,

Israel gently massaged the tight muscles on either side of the indention at the base of her skull, relieved to see how quickly she relaxed.

"It's in my purse." Looking down at her dress, she gave a small shrug. "There wasn't really any place to hide it in this dress, and they asked us to leave them in our lockers."

Oh, please don't... Wait, what am I asking for? Please don't stop massaging my neck because it feels so good? Or please don't keep touching me, or I'm going to make a fool of myself? This damned dress should have pockets. Crickets. Pockets would have been a great distraction. It isn't going to matter in a few seconds because I'm going to burst into flames, and the blasted thing is going to be scorched, anyway.

"The dress is perfect, sweetheart. Seeing the silky expanse of your bareback is sexy as hell. I can hardly wait to see the rest of your creamy skin exposed to my touch." Israel slid his hand slowly down her back. He felt her shiver as her nipples drew into peaks so tight, they drew his eye. Fuck, she was perfect.

"It's refreshing to meet a professional woman who isn't tied to her phone. Your confidence is incredibly attractive, Bristol. Don't ever doubt how heady self-assurance is." Handing her his phone, Israel continued, "Call your phone. That way, you will have my number, and I'll have yours."

With a few quick keystrokes, she made the call. He heard the sound of a phone ringing several times before Bristol's voice mail picked up. Ending the call, she handed his phone back, tilting her head to the side, unasked questions shining in her pretty blue eyes.

Damn, I can't tell him I know he did a background check on me without violating Charlotte's privacy. He could have easily gotten my number. Maybe it's against some rule to use company information for private purposes? Fuck a green duck. Privacy laws are insanely strict and ridiculously lax at the same time, so who the hell knows. I don't want to think about how complicated they are for a business specializing in investigations.

Taking a deep breath, she decided a direct inquiry was best.

"Why do I have the distinct impression you didn't need any help getting my number?"

He admired her ability to phrase the question in a way without any professional compromise. It was also damned interesting, Charlotte trusted her doctor enough to confide that her husband's family did a background investigation.

"Austin is very protective of his lovely wife. It wouldn't have mattered how many of his friends recommended you, he wanted me to make absolutely certain Charlotte and their baby were safe in your care." The pink staining her cheeks made her look more like a college coed than a well-respected physician. Owning a successful medical practice before most women her age completed graduate school was damned impressive. Her accomplished life made it hard to remember how young she was.

"I guess I should be pleased you found me worthy." There was just enough snark in her tone to demand a response. She may as well learn now, the dominant side of his personality was never far below the surface.

"Be careful, Beautiful, snark will always be dealt with. Every challenge will be answered. I'm a Dom to the very depths of my soul. I don't want a twenty-four-seven slave, but I will demand respect. The good news is… I will afford you the same and more." He paused for a few seconds, watching her pulse beat a staccato beat at the base of her throat as her eyes dilated. *Yes, indeed. Bristol Banks is as sexually submissive as any woman I've ever known. Fucking perfect.* "I know this situation has blindsided you. It was a surprise for me as well, though I'm clearly much happier about it than you are." He gave her a reassuring smile as he skimmed his fingers down the side of her beautiful face.

"I'm going to respond to the comment you should have made, rather than the one you said without realizing how it sounded." Her blue eyes flashed for a second before she conceded, giving him a quick nod. "Ordinarily, during an investigation, I would have arranged an accidental meeting. My team and I would have studied your habits, what time you left for work, where you bought your morning coffee, your gym schedule, nights out with your friends—all of those would have given me opportunities to observe you personally. Your background was so clean, it wasn't necessary. Everyone, from your former roommates to your damned childhood nemesis, sang your praises." In hindsight, he wished he'd hadn't deviated from his usual procedure. If he hadn't, perhaps they'd have already moved past her reluctance. He noted she hadn't denied they were fated mates—she'd only said she didn't want it. What he needed to know was why.

"I apologize for being snide. Not because you're a Dom, but because it was unprofessional and rude. I'm thrilled to work with Charlotte, she is a joy, and I would never do anything to jeopardize the trust she's given me… it's a gift. I won't say much because of confidentiality, but I'm certainly free to tell you, I also consider her a friend outside our professional relationship."

"Very tactfully put, Dr. B. I know you are well trained to protect patient confidentiality at all times, but I want you to know anything we discuss will never go any further. You will always be safe, acknowledging someone in my family is your patient."

"Because you'll already know?"

"Yes." Israel gave one quick nod of agreement. "I'll already know. More importantly, I want you to be confident in my promise that anything you say to me about your work will remain completely private. We are fated mates, Bristol. You don't know me and have no reason to trust me... yet. That will change as we grow closer, but it's important for you to know this much upfront. My business centers around confidential information. As a professional, I understand the importance of shielding vital information from prying eyes—whether or not the law requires it." Her eyes widened briefly before he saw her pull in a deep breath.

"I didn't mean to offend you. Protecting my patients is such a huge part of what I do, it's often difficult to remember they are also wives, sisters, and daughters."

"No offense taken, Sweetheart. It's important for us to clear the air and get off on the right foot. Now, let's switch gears. How long have you been a member at Prairie Winds?" Her shoulders relaxed, her posture showing relief at their change of direction.

"A couple of years. I joined shortly after I moved to Austin. I haven't been able to attend as often as I'd like, but I'm hoping that will change soon." When he raised a brow in question, she shrugged. "I've finally brought in another doctor. My practice grew much faster than I thought it would, and it took a long time to find someone I felt confident bringing on board."

"I can't imagine it's easy to find doctors in your field who have any background working with magicals."

"Very difficult. I also wanted someone who understood the BDSM lifestyle. I didn't want a doctor who would bristle when a Dom refused to leave the room during his submissive's examination."

"I don't suppose they teach kink in medical school. Medical professionals who have only experienced vanilla sex wouldn't understand how intensely protective a Dom can be when it comes to protecting what belongs to them." When she nodded, he was pleased to feel her relief. She obviously appreciated his understanding of the challenges she faced.

The guiding tenet of Dominance and submission was always *Safe, Sane, and Consensual*. The words were more than just an abstract concept written into every member-ship contract. They were a promise made between all legitimate BDSM players. But the foundation of any good D/s relationship was communication. He was determined to establish a solid foundation with Bristol—they'd need it to weather the inevitable storms ahead.

They both had demanding careers—working long hours meant they'd have less free time available to spend together. His business often required travel—hell, last year, he'd been out of the office more often than not. Frequent separations were stressful for any relationship, but they were particularly difficult for shifters. Their sexual nature was in overdrive for several weeks after they were first mated, and any significant separation during that time would be particularly painful for both of them.

"There are a lot of special seminars available during a new physician's residency, but I don't remember seeing anything about communication strategies related to interactions with sexual Dominants."

Israel was stunned. He could tell by the sincerity reflected in her expression, she wasn't kidding. Her response wasn't snark, but her sincerity was borderline humorous. Damn, he'd been spending so much time with his artistically inclined siblings, he'd forgotten how literal scientists could be.

Note to self: Remember how you deal with London—do that. The next to youngest Adler had reluctantly taken a step back from her intense research schedule when she'd mated. Now, as the mother of twin sons, she told him she was beginning to return to work. Her goal was to regain some margin of control in her own life, and with any luck, she'd be able to save her sanity. Israel had assumed she was joking until he'd watched her chasing the boys through the Monroe compound a few weeks earlier.

London's mates, Eli and Dr. Evan Monroe, were also twins. They saw the pandemonium as normal and had taken their young sons' antics in stride, laughing when the dynamic duo tried to climb the playground equipment, intent on launching themselves into the air to prove to their harried mother, they could fly. Perhaps knowing one of their dads was a world-renowned orthopedic surgeon provided more of a safety net than the two hellions needed. As much as he'd been looking forward to seeing his nephews this weekend, he'd understood when he heard the young parents left their sons with their grandparents. The pretty blush painting Bristol's cheeks reminded him of the pink he'd watched move over his sister's face when she'd confessed, she wanted time alone with her husbands.

FRAZZLE. I'M SUCH a dork. I can't believe I said that. I may not be ready to be mated, but I don't want the man to think I'm a blooming brainiac with no social skills. Bristol had always been what her friends called a literal geek—she took things at face value, assuming people meant what they said, rather than attributing their words to sarcasm or teasing. *Hell, it's exhausting, trying to sort through every word spoken during a conversation, wondering if it's some kind of puzzle. Who wants to spend time sorting through that nonsense? Probably easy if you grew up with brothers and sisters, constantly yammering some level of bullshit in your ear, morning, noon, and night. Some of us spent all our time with our noses shoved in books, without any time for fun and games.*

"As we learn more about one another, it will get easier, Beautiful."

Israel Adler was wrecking her defenses. The soothing tone of his voice, the gentle way his hand wrapped around her neck—it was seduction on a level Bristol had never experienced. If she didn't get away from him, she'd be begging him to take her before the string quartet finished their first number.

"If we're in a scene, begging may or may not be appreciated. Outside of a defined period of play, you'll never have to beg, Bristol. I will always give you what you need."

It didn't escape her attention, he'd said he would give

her what she needed. During her training, when she first joined the club, she'd been warned there was a difference between what she *wanted* and what she *needed*. She'd never had a D/s relationship but had heard plenty of other subs discussing the distinction.

"I need to get back. I promised to help. It's why I'm here." He kept his hand wrapped around the side of her neck, the pressure of his fingers reminding her he was in control without overwhelming her. The sensation was oddly comforting, and Bristol realized she felt safe when she probably should have felt anything but. When he didn't say anything, she blundered on, "I'm not the sort of person who gets invited to Hollywood superstar's weddings. Heck, I didn't know who was getting married until I got here. We all had to sign nondisclosure agreements... Shitballs with coconut, you probably already knew that."

"Asia and I put the NDAs together, even though we didn't feel they were necessary. We also helped the Wests handpick who they asked to help. You were the first name on the list, Bristol. Charlotte, Asia, and Cat, all listed you as their first choice." She wondered why he'd told her, and he didn't make her wait long for an answer. "It's important you understand where you stand. I'm looking forward to introducing you as my mate. My family is going to be thrilled."

Maybe... maybe not. She wasn't convinced anyone enjoyed socializing with their doctor. In her experience, people valued their physician's opinion, respected their education, trusted their opinion, and appreciated their discretion, but when it came to social events, they were often decidedly chilly.

Bristol found it easier to narrow her practice to patients in the lifestyle and shifters. They weren't uptight about their bodies, but often still had reservations about socializing with their doctor. Nudity was a large part of a shifter's everyday life, so engaging in small talk with someone who'd seen them naked didn't make them particularly uncomfortable. They may be more open than nonmagicals and those in the vanilla world, but there was still an underlying reluctance to cross those invisible social boundaries. When you added in her age, lack of sexual experience, and flakey family, most people backed away quickly. Pulling her thoughts back to the moment, Bristol wondered how long she'd been lost in thought. Israel's indulgent smile told her it had likely been longer than she realized.

Chapter Three

ISRAEL KNEW THE effect he was having on his newly discovered mate. The earthy scent of her arousal circled them in a haze so thick, it was pushing him dangerously close to the edge of his control. Pulling her against him, Israel brushed his lips lightly over hers. Bristol's quickly indrawn breath made him want to kiss her again... and again until he felt the first layer of her reluctance fell away.

"You've been spending time with the wrong people, Bristol. I know the background check seemed intrusive. I'm sorry about that, but it couldn't be helped. If you will stop and think about it, I believe you'll see it's working to your advantage. We already know all the things you're worried about." If he hadn't been completely focused on her, Israel would have missed the brief flash of relief in her eyes.

"As I said before, we don't know each other well enough for you to trust me, but you will. That also goes for my family. They aren't snobs, Beautiful. You're brilliant and beautiful, and I suspect you have a killer sense of humor lurking within. You're going to fit in perfectly. Hell, Asia and London will probably want you to move in." The three women had a lot in common, and he looked forward to seeing how much she enjoyed their company. *Hopefully, they won't scare her off.*

"I haven't met London, but I've read several of her published papers. She does remarkable work. Her discoveries are going to revolutionize the way vaccines are developed and distributed."

Israel wasn't surprised to hear Bristol was already a fan of London's work. Physicians who understood the importance of vaccines but didn't blindly swallow big pharma's narrative loved London's *'err of the side of the angels'* view. Insightful people are always drawn to others who seek the truth. Bristol and London would likely become fast friends.

"Traditionally, scientists were easily compromised because their research was funded by big pharmaceutical companies. Government oversight was minimal at best until you started wading through the bureaucracy of the FDA. Every stage is a money game." Bristol's passion for her patients' care was easy to hear in her voice.

"Holy shit, if you don't claim her, I'm going to adopt her. She just spoke to my heart." Israel looked over his shoulder and grinned when he saw London standing behind him. Flanked by Asia, Paris, Catalina, and Brooklyn, the group would have seemed intimidating if they hadn't all been smiling like cats who'd just swallowed the proverbial canaries. London always reminded him of a sprite, a petite ball of barely contained energy. She'd calmed down some since she'd become a mother, but without the boys here this weekend, the old London was shining through.

"Come on, Bristol, Israel has kept you to himself long enough. Time for some fun. Tobi is going to teach us line dancing." As the oldest of the girls, Asia rarely missed an opportunity to take charge. She and London stepped forward, each grabbing one of Bristol's elbows, intent on leading her away.

"Hold on, ladies." When Israel moved to intervene, London elbowed him aside.

"Back off, Barney. We'll bring her back after we're finished enjoying ourselves. Austin is looking for you, anyway. He can't keep Charlotte in her chair. She wants to walk because she's having cramps. Austin is bitching about her being fifteen months pregnant and swearing he's going to tie her to a chair if she doesn't sit down and put her feet up."

"Cramps? What kind of cramps? Where is she? Come on, let's go." Israel watched his mate slip out of her heels and take off running with the fluid grace of a shifter. He smiled when she instinctively ran to one of the small enclosed areas where a small group was gathered. He stopped to scoop up her shoes, grateful to be able to do a small act of service, making their connection seem more intimate than it had a few seconds ago.

"You are fucking pathetic, man. Shoes? Small act of service? Shit, you should be forced to surrender your Man Card." Israel didn't need to turn to know Luke Grayson was standing beside him. Brooklyn Adler's husband had two incredible skills—a gifted telepath and computer hacker extraordinaire. Everybody Israel knew wondered if the two talents were connected, but it was a chicken and egg argument, Israel considered a waste of time attempting to unravel. Anybody with an IQ above dull-normal knew the two were indelibly linked.

"Fuck you, Grayson. Didn't anybody tell you it's rude

to eavesdrop?" Israel didn't remember there being an exemption for telepathic snooping.

"Sure, all the time. I just don't give a shit. Besides, you think loud, so it's on you." Luke flashed an unrepentant grin and shrugged. "Come on, we don't want to miss the action. I hope Denali doesn't mind having her wedding day overshadowed by a baby."

"In this family, the odds of having a special occasion derailed by another family member are increasing exponentially." Israel couldn't imagine Denali being upset but decided to check in with her just in case. As he approached where she was standing with Kenz, all he felt was concern for her new sister-in-law. Pulling her into a hug, he held her until he finally felt her take a deep breath.

"That's better." He set her back alongside her new husband but kept his hand on her shoulder. "How are you doing, sweetness? Unfortunately, this is one of the perils of a large family."

"Perils? I don't understand what you mean." He could feel the confusion pulsing around her.

"I'm sure Charlotte is worried she is upstaging your big day. I can't imagine she'd have come today if she knew this would happen." Denali's expression morphed from confusion to horror.

"Are you kidding? This is the best wedding present anyone could ever receive. I'm getting a niece or nephew. This adds another layer of joy to the most amazing wedding day ever. We'll be able to celebrate forever, and the whole family will never forget our anniversary. Seriously, how much better can it get?" Israel pressed a chaste kiss against her forehead before turning to Kenz.

"She is perfect. Take very good care of her." Turning his attention to the sudden shift in the energy behind him, Israel focused on his mate, grateful he could easily tap into her thoughts.

Shit. We'll never get Charlotte to the hospital in time. I hope the club's first aid station is well stocked. She sounded stressed but not panicked. Israel wanted to reach out to her telepathically, but he didn't want to be a distraction.

"Let's get Charlotte moved inside, so we can minimize the disruption to Kensington and Denali's reception." She'd been speaking to several of the people gathered around Charlotte. When Austin started to lift his wife, Bristol put her hand on his forearm. "I'd like you to stay for a moment, please. Walking will help her muscles relax, and I'd like to speak with you privately. I have a request, and I know everyone will do a great job getting Charlotte settled." Austin's eyes widened in surprise, but he nodded before giving his mate a quick kiss and assuring her he'd be right behind her.

Bristol moved, so she was standing directly in front of Austin, her bare feet a few inches apart, and her hands held loosely at her sides. Her body language exuded a level of easy confidence he knew was well-practiced. Israel smiled, knowing she was making a deliberate effort to put Austin at ease. Her calm demeanor and cool professionalism made it easier for everyone around her to do what needed to be done.

"Austin, I know this isn't the way you and Charlotte planned for your baby to make his or her grand entrance, but I want you to know I'm going to do everything I can to make certain everything goes smoothly. Charlotte is young and healthy." Bristol's calm was broken for few seconds by a broad grin. "These are the times when being a shifter pays off in spades." Calm surrounded her once again, the face Israel was quickly coming to recognize as her professional persona sliding effortlessly back into place.

"Your job—*your only job*—is to support your wife. Everything else is on me. I want to make certain you understand that before we walk in there. It's going to get a little crazy at times, and you're accustomed to being in charge—you have to let that go for a while. I want you to keep your focus on Charlotte."

Turning to Israel, she asked, "Can you please get my car keys from my locker—number twenty-eight. I need the black bag from the back seat of my car." Israel nodded and took off jogging toward the club's back entrance. He'd have the attendant open the locker if he couldn't get it open himself. Behind him, he heard his mate tell Austin it was time to go. Bristol sprinted past him. Austin's muttered curses made Israel laugh as they entered the club together.

"Fucking hell, she's fast. Where on earth are her shoes?" Israel held up the strappy sandals and grinned.

"We're out of shape, brother. We both work too hard and exercise too little. That was damned humbling."

BRISTOL WAS PLEASED to find the first aid station at the club was better equipped than some emergency rooms she'd worked in. The area wasn't particularly well-equipped for childbirth, but she'd made do with a lot less. When Bristol saw Israel step into the open door, holding her bag, she moved quickly to where he waited patiently.

"Thanks so much..." Before she could say anything else, he pulled her against his chest, holding her until she took a deep breath.

"You're welcome, Beautiful. I'll be right outside the door if you need anything else—even if it's nothing more than a hug." The sudden rush of emotion she felt was so unexpected, she wasn't sure what to do with it. Sentiment had never been a significant part of her life. For so many years, everything had centered on her education, and she'd always known setting aside feelings would be a critical part of being able to make fact-based decisions for patients.

"When my niece or nephew finally makes their appearance, I'll be here waiting. If you think I'm going to let you fade into the background, you should think again."

She nodded numbly. Part of her knew she needed to get back to Charlotte, but her body's off-the-chart physical reaction made it almost impossible to remember anything beyond a crazy desire to be touched by this man. When he finally took a step back, Bristol shook her head, chastising herself to get her head back down out of the damned clouds.

"Go." Israel gave her a quick kiss and smiled. "I can hear my brother freaking out."

Twenty minutes later, Bristol swiped sweat from her brow, wishing somebody would turn on a damned fan. She was going to be dehydrated by the time Austin and Charlotte's baby decided to make an appearance. *I'm on it, sweetness. Hang on while I find the thermostat.* As startled as she was by the reminder Israel could hear her thoughts, Bristol felt tears of gratitude burn her eyes when cool air moved through the room.

"Praise be the Goddess of Air Conditioning. I was two heartbeats from dying of heatstroke," Charlotte gasped between her contractions. They were coming so close together, there was only a few seconds between them. "Why did I think I could do this without drugs? Crap on a prickly cactus, I'm not ready to be a mother. Don't you have to pass some sort of class to be a parent? I didn't even get a syllabus, let alone take the final. Fuckity fuck, I barely passed the exam to get my driver's license. I changed my mind. Please send the baby back. I'll get one later—when there are drugs. Yes, that is a great idea. Poke the baby with the head the size of a fricking watermelon back into his or her papa."

"Little Star, you are pushing your luck. Dr. B. said you couldn't be held responsible for anything said during delivery, but it would be unwise to take advantage of my generosity." Austin's voice took on a tone any submissive would recognize. The man was a Dom to the tips of his toes. Charlotte was busy pushing, but the glare she leveled at her husband was easy to read.

"The exemption stands, Mr. Adler. I make certain all fathers know, especially the Doms. You have to understand the rules going in, or you get to pace in the waiting room." Bristol was only half-concentrating on the conversation. She was much more interested in the dark head of hair inching closer. Damn, this baby was going to be the envy of the nursery. "Your wife is going through childbirth, without the epidural block she'd planned on having—she has more than earned that grace."

"I'm never having sex again. Never. It's too dangerous.

I should have read the book. No more mindless passion for me... I'm going to become a nun." The shocked look on Austin Adler's face was priceless—too bad, Bristol didn't have time to enjoy it.

"One more push, Mama. You'll have a baby in your arms before you know it. Charlotte, you have been amazing. It's been a long time since I've had a first-time mother deliver naturally without shredding their husband. I'm sure Austin is damned proud of you." *Grab it with both hands, Papa. I just threw you a huge lifeline.*

Austin wasn't the only one who'd done their home-work. Bristol checked him out when Charlotte first expressed an interest in becoming a patient. Austin's business reputation was akin to local legend. He'd taken his parents' failing oil enterprise and turned it into a phenome-nal success. Adler Oil was diversifying and growing so fast, articles about it were outdated almost as soon as they were printed. His success wasn't an accident—the man was widely regarded as a brilliant businessman.

He walked confidently through the opening she'd giv-en him.

"I don't think I've ever been more impressed with any-one, Little Star. Dr. B is right, you are amazing, and I'm humbled to see what you have endured to bring our child into the world." He helped her lift up, so she'd have more leverage for the final push, kissing her brow and whisper-ing endearments Bristol tried to tune out. Seconds later, the problem was solved when the cries of baby Adler filled the room.

"Congratulations, you have a very handsome son. I don't think he is particularly happy with me at the moment, but I promise to make it up to him." She wiped the squirming little boy off as much as she could before placing him on his mama's chest. "You three enjoy a few minutes of bonding while I finish up things down below. We'll have you ready for transport in no time."

She would ride to the hospital in the ambulance as a precaution and hope like holy hell, she could persuade a taxi driver to bring her back to the club to pick up her car. Last night's full moon meant she'd spent all night delivering babies, only catching a short nap before she'd headed to Prairie Winds to help with the wedding reception. At this point, she was running on caffeine and a prayer.

Maybe I'll catch a cab home and worry about my car later… a lot later. Damn, I'm pooped.

Chapter Four

ISRAEL TRIED TO catch up with Bristol before she slipped into the back of the ambulance with Charlotte and the new baby but missed her. When he called Austin, his brother answered on the first ring.

"Congratulations, big brother. How are you holding up?" Israel already knew Charlotte and baby Marshall were doing well, but the man who'd held the family together after the death of their parents was looking a little shell shocked.

"I'm still trying to process the whole thing. One minute, I'm enjoying a glass of champagne, toasting my brother and new sister-in-law, the next, I find out my wife's in labor. I think when all the dust settles, I'm going to discover she'd been in labor for hours but failed to mention it because she didn't want to miss the wedding."

"Probably. Although I doubt, she thought little Marshall would decide to kick things into high gear. Don't be too hard on her. Remember, she's given you the best gift you've ever received, and she did it without any pain relief." Israel could feel Austin's pride in both the birth of his son and his wife's bravery.

"You're right about cutting her some slack but wrong

about the gift. *She* is the best gift I've ever received—everything that happens after she came into my life is icing on a very sweet and perfect cake. I'm deeply indebted to Bristol." Austin took a deep breath, sighing softly before continuing. "She kept me from making a huge mistake. I was on the cusp of ruining a remarkable experience. Charlotte would have forgiven me—eventually—but I would have never forgiven myself. It was damned humbling to be reminded I can't always force people to toe the line."

"Being at the club probably didn't help. Your role in this environment is well-established. It's okay to be grateful, but don't wallow in what could have been. It will keep you from enjoying the joy of the moment." Israel wondered if Austin realized he'd let out a breath in a rush of self-awareness.

"You're right. Thank you."

"I'm following you into town. Bristol is exhausted. From what I could pick up, she's been up for the better part of thirty-six hours. She left her car at the club, and I want to make sure she gets home safely. Give me a heads up when she finishes with Charlotte. I don't want to miss her."

"Her home or yours?" Austin laughed before plunging ahead. "Hell, never mind, I already know the answer. She is a strong, independent woman—tread carefully. Don't smother her. I can't see that ending well for you."

Israel knew his brother was right but had no illusions about his ability to hold back his desire to protect his mate. It didn't matter he hadn't formally claimed her—she belonged to him.

Sitting in the waiting room two hours later, Israel was

relieved when his phone vibrated in his pocket. The text message from Austin was short and sweet. *Heads up.* Moving closer to the door, he heard the nurses talking about Bristol. Before he could find out what he wanted to know, an automatic door opened down the hall, and his eyes locked on Bristol as a wave of physical and emotional exhaustion hit him like a freight train. Stepping forward, Israel opened his arms and felt like his heart would burst when she didn't hesitate to walk into his embrace.

"I'm so tired. Thank Goddess, my apartment is nearby. I'll be able to stay awake long enough to drive that far." *Hopefully.*

"Your car is at the club, Beautiful." He tightened his hold when she sagged, fearing her knees were going to fold out from under her.

"Damn, I forgot. I'll call a cab. Thanks for sticking around to say goodbye." The words sounded sincere, but her emotions were telling an entirely different story.

"Bristol, it's important you are honest with yourself and with me." Israel gave her a quick squeeze before releasing her to look into her pale blue eyes. Using the pads of his fingers, he smoothed back the loose strands of her hair, fascinated by the silky feel of the white-blonde tresses.

"I can hardly wait to see your hair fanned out over my bare chest, your eyes half-lidded from satisfaction, rather than the exhaustion I see in them now." It was time to move on. She was precariously close to falling asleep on her feet. Turning her toward the exit, he kept an arm around her waist. He wanted her close, and her fatigue gave him the perfect excuse. Steering Bristol out the door, he was glad he'd kept his hands on her when she stumbled several yards from his car. Without missing a step, Israel leaned down and scooped her into his arms.

"Oh pickles, this is embarrassing. I shouldn't let you carry me, but to be honest, I'm not sure I can make it to the cab stop."

He hated hearing the utter exhaustion in her voice. Hell, how many times had she pushed herself to this point and beyond with no one to watch her back?

"Can you do something for me, Bristol? Will you let me take care of you tonight?" Before he could walk the short distance to his car, Israel felt her tears soaking through his shirt. *Talk to me, Beautiful.* He'd deliberately used telepathic communication, hoping the deeper level of intimacy would make it easier for her to admit what he could feel coming off her in waves.

While he'd waited for her, Israel had pulled the file his team had done on her from the company server to refresh his memory. She'd had a horrific childhood compared to his. Things appeared to improve—marginally—after she moved in with an unmarried high school science teacher. By the time the older woman died a couple of years later, Bristol had already been ready to attend college.

Wondering if anyone in the deceased teacher's circle of friends could provide information, Israel did a quick search and was shocked by what he found—or, more specifically, what he didn't find. The woman hadn't existed prior to the year Bristol started high school.

The prestigious university Bristol chose didn't want to lose their child protégé, so they'd made special housing arrangements for the young girl. Interviews with her fellow classmates and professors all echoed the same sentiment—

what was supposed to be a charitable concession turned out to be horribly isolating. Everyone they interviewed mentioned how sorry they'd felt for her. If she wasn't in class, working in the lab, or studying in the library, Bristol was locked in her own wing of one of the smaller dormitories. The Dean had insisted she be protected, but her safety had come at an enormous emotional cost.

Unbelievably, Bristol finished graduate school before she had been old enough to drive, which meant she'd been forced to walk everywhere. Hell, she'd attended Harvard, and it was fucking cold in Boston during the winter. No wonder she'd moved to Texas.

He'd done a background check on a Harvard Medical School professor several years ago and knew how damned relentless the cold wind was as it swept across the campus in January. Cold, inhospitable hell was how Israel described it to his executive assistant when he'd returned home. Geneva had chuckled and rolled her eyes. She'd warned him to assign the investigation to one of the newer members of the team, and the unspoken reminder was dancing in her eyes.

"You're going to have to get a handle on delegating before you find a woman, or you're never going to keep one. You work all the time."

She was right. Hell, he'd only recently started delegating more of the responsibility to Cleveland, and he was his damned brother.

Settling his exhausted mate in his car gave Israel an odd sense of familiarity, almost like a preview of coming attractions. In a flash of insight, he knew this wouldn't be the last time he carried his sweet, overworked mate out of the hospital. He planned to help her learn how to bring more balance into her life. Israel rolled his eyes at the irony of him teaching his mate to work less. Bristol was young, but she'd been on her own for a long time, so it would be hard for her to loosen the tight grip she kept on her control. It wouldn't be an easy transition, and he hoped she'd learn to trust him sooner rather than later.

Reaching over her, Israel fastened her seat belt, then brushed his lips across hers and reclined her seat. "Rest, Beautiful. We'll be home in no time."

"I'm just going to close my eyes for a few minutes." *I liked the kiss. Wish I wasn't so tired. I wanted more.*

Smiling to himself, Israel closed the door and moved to the driver's side. Slipping behind the wheel, he was surprised to see Bristol had pulled off the skull cap she'd been wearing, the brightly colored cloth clutched loosely in her hand. Taking her hand in his, Israel placed the cap in his lap before leaning close and pulling her fingers to his lips. *Rest, Dr. B, I'm going to take such good care of you, you'll never want to leave.*

Driving to Adler Oil didn't take long. This early in the pre-dawn morning, traffic was practically nonexistent. Israel enjoyed watching the soft amber light from the overhead streetlights fan over his sleeping passenger. The light danced over her wild tumble of blonde hair, glinting off the waves, giving her an ethereal appearance.

Israel wanted to commit the moment to memory. He kept her hand in his, enjoying the feel of her slender fingers against his palm. Parking in the private parking lot under his family's building, he took a moment to enjoy the view. Bristol reminded him of the classic pin-up girls of the 1940s.

She was perfect. Damn, he'd loved having her in his arms. She was a soft armful. He'd never been attracted to women who were supermodel thin, preferring those with breasts and curves.

The pictures in her file didn't begin to do her justice. Bristol Banks was gorgeous on the outside, and the past few hours, she'd proven she was even more attractive on the inside. Sitting outside the club's first aid station, he'd tried hard to filter what he was hearing from her. Israel hadn't wanted to know all the details of his sister-in-law's childbirth experience, but he'd wanted to track how well Bristol was holding up once it became clear she was running on fumes.

Moving around the car, he made a quick call upstairs to where the night crew manned a large bank of monitors. His staff not only helped secure all the public areas of Adler Oil, they also watched for any signs of trouble at any of the clients' properties. The guys in the control room could operate the elevators with a few keystrokes, and Israel wanted to be able to carry his precious cargo without worrying about juggling her to insert key cards or tap in codes.

"Come on, Beautiful, let's get you upstairs and settled." She barely stirred when he lifted her from the car. The warmth of her soft sigh moved over the side of his neck, sending a surge of blood to his cock. Dandy, just what he needed his staff to see—him sporting a hard-on as he carried an unconscious woman into his suite.

It didn't take long to get her out of her scrubs and into the shower. Israel decided the loose-fitting clothing was his new second favorite attire. He'd always favor short dresses worn without panties, but drawstring pants weren't bad. Easy access was at the top of his priority list. Thankfully, Bristol was a natural submissive, which meant she responded perfectly to his instructions spoken in his Dom voice.

"I can't believe I'm in the shower with a man I barely know. Frickity frack, I don't even know who's shower this is." The words were spoken out loud—barely—but she hadn't bothered to open her eyes.

"It's my shower, my precious, exhausted mate. I wanted to take care of you, and I can do it better here." Reaching around her to turn off the water, he pulled a towel from the warming rack. She sighed in contentment when he wrapped the thick bath sheet around her.

Spoiling. Flogger. Babies are sweet, but they sure like to put a kink in my kink.

Just when he thought he was winning the battle to keep his unruly cock under control, she mentions kink, sending a surge of blood south.

You're playing with fire, baby. He sat her between his splayed legs on the padded bench at the end of the bed to comb the tangles from her hair. Pulling the long locks into a loose braid, he tied the bottom with an elastic tie, one of his sisters had left at some point. The suite he was currently using had been occupied by several of the Adler siblings at various times, so the bathroom drawers held a strange mix of abandoned accessories.

"Come on, Beautiful, let's get you comfortable." After settling her in bed, Israel took time to make sure the suite was secured, throwing the extra lock that would ensure none of his siblings could enter using their master key.

They all had an electronic key, which allowed them access to any Adler owned space, but there were also special locks in case someone wanted privacy. Slipping between the cool sheets, Israel pulled his mate close, closing his arms around her. Bristol fit perfectly against him, her back pressed against his chest, skin to skin, shoulders to hips.

The position was comfortable and torture at the same time. Her scent surrounded him, and when he leaned forward to skim his lips over the top of her shoulder, the urge to claim her was almost more than he could resist. Israel knew it would be easy to get a yes from her—hell, she was so tired, she would likely agree to anything that would get him to leave her alone, so she could sleep. But as much as he *wanted her*, he also wanted her to make an informed decision.

Her mind went silent within seconds, and he knew she was asleep—it took him a lot longer to let go. It had been an amazing twenty-four hours. Kensington and Denali were finally legally man and wife, Austin and Charlotte had a healthy son, thanks to the woman in his arms, and he'd found his mate.

Fucking amazing.

CLOVIA WILLIAMS WATCHED Master Israel lead Dr. Banks out of the hospital and frowned. She was hidden in the shadows, but the darkness wouldn't have mattered if the wind hadn't been in her favor. The scene Clovia shared with Master Israel had been months ago, but as a shifter, he would recognize her from scent alone. To boost Israel's scent memory, Clovia had made certain he got regular reminders. Standing near vents when he was playing at the club, spraying the door handle of his car with her perfume, and tucking a perfume-soaked piece of fabric in his locker at the club were a few of the ways she'd helped imprint sensory receptors with reminders of their time together. Every time she remembered the night he'd shown her all the ways a Dom could please a submissive, her body launched into sexual overdrive. It had been their only night together—so far.

Since Clovia's scene with Master Israel, he'd proven why he was a sought-after tracker. The damned man had been as elusive as smoke, drifting in and out of the Prairie Winds Club. Asking some of the other submissives at the club about him had been discouraging, but Clovia wasn't one to give in easily. Israel Adler was more than a skilled sexual Dominant; he was also a highly regarded tracker. His reputation among the multiple shifter packs in North America was impeccable. He was widely considered by many to be Austin Adler's chosen successor, despite being the seventh in age. Clovia had done her research after she'd realized Master Israel was her mate.

Additionally, all the Adler siblings were loaded. Not only were their trust funds damned impressive, thanks to Austin Adler's remarkable leadership, they'd each become incredibly successful in their own right.

Clovia had enjoyed several scenes at the club with Austin before he'd mated with Charlotte. They'd enjoyed one another's company, but there had never been any question, it was nothing more than mutual pleasure. When he'd seen her tonight, Master Austin had been polite, acknowledging her in the same way you would any casual business acquaintance. Clovia understood... hell, she'd done the same to Masters and fellow submissives, she encountered outside the club. But it was different when Israel treated her as though they'd never met. She'd been hurt and angry when Master Israel ignored her.

His unique, masculine scent had alerted her to his presence as soon as he stepped out of the elevator. He'd stopped in to check on his new nephew and sister-in-law, given his brother a congratulatory hug, inquired about Dr. B, then one of her co-workers directed him to the waiting room beyond the security doors. It was a testament to his connections, he'd been given access to the employee elevator, and she'd wondered why he was waiting for Dr. B—until she'd seen him carrying the physician to his car.

Clovia had watched Master Israel at the club for almost a year before she finally got the opportunity to scene with him. His touch was magic, but she'd never seen him look at any sub the way he looked at Bristol Banks. Why was he so enthralled with Bristol when it was so obvious, he belonged to her? Where the hell was he taking her? Clovia knew where Dr. B lived, but the taillights of Israel's car turned in the opposite direction. Maybe he was taking the doctor back to Prairie Winds to get her car. Clovia was still pissed she hadn't been invited to help with the wedding. She rarely worked weekend shifts but was drafted to help when her supervisor failed to schedule additional staff during the full moon. Hell, the woman had only been a labor and delivery nurse for a fucking decade—you'd think she'd know the ropes by now.

Stepping out of the shadows, Clovia made her way

back inside. There wasn't anything she could do about the situation now—she still had at least another hour before she could go home. Maybe things would make more sense after she got a good night's sleep. Clovia would make some calls tomorrow and find out what happened after the wedding. Hell, as famous as Kensington Adler was, it may well be on the damned news.

One of the other subs would know whether Master Israel took Dr. B back to her car. Fucking hell, Clovia finally found the man she knew was destined to be hers, then had to watch him carry another woman to his car. There had to be a logical explanation—she just needed to find out what it was.

Chapter Five

B RISTOL COULDN'T REMEMBER the last time she'd been this comfortable. The sheets sliding over her heated skin were cool and so smooth, they felt like silk. The fabric was a luxury she never indulged in for herself. She wanted to stretch, just to see how it felt caressing her bare ass.

Wait. Bare? I'm naked? I can't be naked. I always wear a sleep shirt and panties to bed. Sometimes, I wear socks and yoga pants, but naked? Nope.

"Go back to sleep, Beautiful. You don't have to be anywhere today, and your body needs rest. You are naked because I want to feel your warmth pressed against mine."

She didn't know what time it was, but the room was cool and dark—perfect. She was more comfortable than she'd ever been in her cheap bed, but her bladder was demanding attention. Damn.

"Two minutes. You better be back in two minutes. Don't doubt for one minute I will come and get you."

Scrambling out of his embrace, Bristol didn't worry about flashing her bare bits in Israel's direction—no doubt he'd seen more memorable asses. He'd seemed more than a little interested in her, but standing on the other side of the bathroom door after she'd finished, the old insecurities started to resurface.

She embraced the kinky side of her personality, but her open-minded view stopped short of feeling confident about her naked body. It didn't matter how much time she spent, toiling away in the hospital's gym, Bristol had too many curves to be considered slender. Crickets, two of those well-rounded, bouncy features would have been on full display when she'd sprinted across Israel's bedroom a minute ago.

The door opened with a whoosh, startling her, and she let out a quick shriek of surprise.

"Time's up."

She probably should have been scandalized, seeing Israel in all his naked glory, but the truth was, she was too fascinated to be shocked. His cock was wide awake, reaching almost to his belly button and... huge. As a physician, Bristol understood the mechanics of sex and the body's ability to adapt and stretch... but there were limits. *There have to be limits. Right?*

A significant portion of her work time was spent watching women push babies the size of small watermelons through a channel ordinarily the width of a couple of fingers. She was always amazed by the human body—frighteningly frail and remarkably resilient at the same time. Truthfully, it was shocking humans hadn't died off centuries earlier.

"Your mind whirls very quickly, Dr. B." He sounded as if he was trying to keep the amusement out of his voice. She knew she'd cycled through several topics in the time it took him to take a couple of deep breaths. Hell, the way her gaze locked on his morning woody made her wish he would just get on with it and fuck her into a stupor.

"Come back to bed. The sun won't be up for hours, and I already know you're off today." She started to ask how he knew she was off today, but he shook his head, laced their fingers together, and tugged her back to bed. "I wasn't snooping into your private business—although I'll never take that off the table where your health and safety are concerned. You were muttering in your sleep, talking about how you were looking forward to a weekend off. We'll talk later. You need sleep, and my self-control is not without limits, Beautiful. Your scent is making me so hard, I'm afraid my damned cock is going to split its skin. The sleep-tousled hair, pink blush, and inquisitive eyes are going to move this along much faster than you're ready for, Bristol."

Fuckity fuck. She could feel the heated blush moving over her so quickly, it felt like she'd been dipped in liquid fire. She'd never been comfortable with her body, but she took a deep breath, grateful his expression didn't hold any judgment. The only thing she saw in his eyes was concern and desire. He got into the enormous bed and held the cover open for her.

"Come. Lie down next to me, so we can go back to sleep before the last thread of my fraying control snaps. There are only two ways for that to end, Beautiful. I'll either fuck you until neither of us wants to move for hours, or we'll go to the playroom." His eyes darkened, and she assumed her ass would pay the price if that was the path she chose.

Letting her eyes drift around the room, she wondered if there were any shirts in the nearby chest of drawers. A t-shirt would help her sleep, anything to cover her bare breasts and ass. "Don't even think about it, Bristol." Heaving a sigh, she got back in bed and laid stiffly at the edge of the mattress.

"I don't think so, Beautiful." This time his words were more of a growl than coaxing. Wrapped around her waist, Israel's hands almost spanned her thick mid-section. "Thick? You are going to spend a lot of time over my lap if you keep this up. You are perfect. Contrary to what many women believe, most men aren't attracted to toothpicks. We appreciate curves and want to be able to feel your softness beneath us."

Settling her against him, Israel smiled when she rested her head against his bicep. His cock laid between the cheeks of her ass as though it had every right to be there. His palm pressed against the underside of her breast, and he fought back a moan when he felt her nipple peaking against the pad of his fingers. Splaying his other hand over her lower abdomen, Israel smiled to himself as her scent moved over him in slow, lapping waves as her skin heated beneath his touch.

"You are so responsive. I know you are fighting it, and that makes it all the sweeter. I can hardly wait until you belong to me. I'm looking forward to tying you to my bed and waking you with my tongue, tracing the folds of your delectable pussy. Maybe I'll finger you until you're nice and slick, then slip inside you before going to sleep."

"Normally, I'd appreciate your take on a bedtime story, but in this case, it seems more like teasing. At least my dreams will be a lot more interesting now… if I can get the visual out of my head and my heart to stop pounding." She felt his chest vibrate against her back and let herself slip back into the peaceful oblivion before sleep. Knowing she'd amused one of the club's Masters made her smile.

Bristol learned at an early age to keep the lighter side of her personality hidden from all but her closest friends. If she joked around in public, she could almost count out the seconds until the blonde bimbo jokes started. Being younger than her colleagues hadn't helped—they'd usually discounted her ideas without even giving them considera- tion, citing her age or chalking up anything outside their comfort zone as the rantings of a blonde ding-bat. It had been humiliating, and she discovered early, it was easier to maintain a professional distance.

Israel made her feel... she didn't know exactly how to describe it... something akin to important. He focused on her when they were together and seemed to want to learn more about her rather than simply trying to find a flaw to exploit. Sighing to herself, Bristol let herself float deeper into the twilight before true sleep.

Frickity frack, I'm not ready to be mated, and Israel Adler is going to be damned hard to resist. Why does fate always open the perfect door when I'm not ready?

REMARKABLE. THE WOMAN was so much more than he'd dared dream fate would send his way. It seemed greedy to ask for a woman as brilliant and beautiful as his sisters and sisters-in-law, but that was exactly what he got. The Adler siblings might have lost their parents too soon, but the great Goddess was showering them with blessings now.

Israel couldn't remember a time when being telepathic had been more important. He and Luke had sat at the hotel bar after Austin and Charlotte tied the knot, wondering how in the hell men could conceivably understand women if they couldn't eavesdrop on their thoughts.

Refining the plan he'd been working on was easy. He just had to keep reminding himself it was more important to establish a good foundation with Bristol than to rush a relationship he knew would last the rest of his life. There wasn't a doubt in the world he could seduce her—Bristol wasn't as sexually experienced as he was. Hell, she wasn't experienced in anything other than her chosen field, but she was fucking brilliant as an OBGYN. She'd already admitted to herself she was susceptible to his charm, but he wasn't willing to trade one night of pleasure for the trust he knew it would take for them to build a future together.

Staring into the darkened room, letting his thoughts wander, Israel saw his phone flash on the nightstand. He'd silenced the device but had obviously forgotten to turn the damned thing over, so it didn't light up the damned room every time a message popped up. Curious who would send a message at this hour, he reached for it, then wished he hadn't.

What is your connection to Clovia Williams?

Austin's question caught him off guard. The name sounded familiar, but Israel wasn't sure why. He would ask his brother for details later. Israel didn't want to risk disturbing the woman sleeping peacefully in his arms by tapping out a response. Whatever the issue, it would have to wait until he had a few free minutes.

When Israel woke up, the fingers of one hand were

closed around Bristol's breast, and his other hand was spread over her lower abdomen, the tips of his fingers pressed against her pubic bone. The heat from her pussy was luring him closer, but he was determined to stick to his new plan.

Bristol's mind was still quiet, blissfully unaware of how her body was expressing its need for his touch. Resisting the urge to roll her budding nipple between the pads of his fingers was difficult, but fighting the temptation to slip the tips of his fingers between her legs was harder than anything he'd had to do in a long time. He knew the moment she woke—her entire body stiffened.

Leaving his hand over her breast, Israel skimmed his other hand up until his arm wrapped possessively around Bristol's waist. Giving her a quick hug before releasing her, Israel moved back until he could sit on the edge of the bed. He didn't have to wait long for her to turn to face him. Goddess above, she was even more stunning in the morning. Her sleepy eyes and disheveled hair, a riot of blonde waves, made him long for the time when he'd see this view every morning. Sometime during the night, the loose braid he'd done in her hair had come undone, though he wasn't sure how, when she'd barely moved all night.

"Thank you for taking such good care of me last night." A pink stain of embarrassment colored her cheeks.

"It was my pleasure, Beautiful. Your safety will always be my number one priority. It would have been irresponsible for me to let you try to get home on your own." On some level, she trusted him enough to let go last night. He wasn't naïve enough to believe she couldn't have got home on her own. Would she have been vulnerable? Absolutely and that was the reason he'd been determined to escort her.

"I don't usually have such a strong reaction to fatigue. Honestly, after medical school, internship, and residency, I would have sworn I was immune to exhaustion."

"You trusted me to keep you safe. Your mind may not understand, but your heart does. I know you don't want to be tied down with a mate." He held up his hand when she started to argue. "Save yourself the swats, lying will earn. You need to can the denial, Bristol. I'm an empath, and my skills are even more enhanced with you." Her eyes widened, and he wanted to laugh at how quickly she mentally reviewed their interactions since he'd approached her at the wedding reception.

"Come back to me, Sweetheart." Bristol blinked a couple of times as if she were trying to refocus her attention. He could see where others might mistake her blank look for something other than her mind moving at warp speed. She'd endured a lot of heartache because she was brilliant. He was anxious for her to get to know his family, who would appreciate her sharp mind. London would have a unique understanding of being academically accelerated.

"Come on." Holding out his hand, Israel nodded his approval when she took it without hesitation. "Let's make breakfast and talk." When her eyes flickered to the master bath, he chuckled. "Do what you need to do, then join me. You'll find button-down shirts in the closet. You can wear one of the white ones with one button closed. No panties. There is a new toothbrush in the top right drawer. Don't stall. I *will* know." He grabbed a pair of boxers on his way to the door, leaving her standing in the middle of the room, staring as he walked naked out of the room.

Israel wasn't concerned about using the guest bathroom since it was kept well stocked with extra toiletries. Even though there were other suites available for visiting guests, his brothers and sisters often opted to stay with him if they were in town. He made a quick stop before moving to the kitchen, barely having enough time to get the coffee started before he noticed Bristol standing by the breakfast bar. It looked as if she'd tried to tame her hair, but the sexy waves reminded him of the expression 'organized chaos.' Her face was scrubbed clean, and her cheeks were pink with embarrassment from her lack of clothing. *Gorgeous.* Waving her to one of the bar stools, he turned back to the stove.

"I'm hungry, so I'll make breakfast while you tell me about yourself." She pulled her lower lip between her teeth, biting down hard enough, he hoped she wouldn't break the skin. "Before you ask, yes, I re-read the investigative report my company did on you, but I want to know about the woman behind the diplomas. Let's try this... What was it like, starting your own practice in a new city? How long did it take you to get patients, etc.?" He didn't know how the process worked, so it was a legitimate inquiry.

With a quick nod, Bristol explained the process of getting her medical credentials transferred to Texas. He was impressed with the deal she'd negotiated with a couple of medical facilities, agreeing to refer patients to their facilities in return for the use of office space in their busier clinics.

"What made you build your own facility?" He'd never wanted the added hassle of owning the building. Operations and sales were Bronx's areas of expertise, not Israel's.

"Financial security. Medical centers are struggling, and I couldn't risk getting sucked into the money drain. Building is insanely expensive, and the maintenance is a nightmare, but being able to control my overhead makes all the difference. I don't have to worry about kissing the asses of shareholders or paying dividends, and I'm able to pass more of the profits on to my employees in the form of bonuses and other incentives."

He was impressed with her business savvy and told her so.

"Thank you. When I graduated, one of my biggest worries was the business side of operating a medical practice. Charlotte told me I should talk to your brother, Bronx. She said he is an incredible businessman, but it seems to me, you are all remarkably successful."

"You're right about my siblings' success. We've been damned lucky." When she frowned, he laughed. "Why do I think my earlier 'be honest with everyone, especially yourself' speech is about to come back and bite me in the ass?"

"I understand humility… but calling everything you've done *luck* is pushing that boundary way past the point of believability."

Israel didn't try to hold back his laughter. She was right, and he didn't mind being called out—unless they were in a scene. He watched her closely as she seemed to study him with matching intensity.

"I'm calling bullshit, Israel. As far as I can tell, all the Adler siblings are intelligent and driven. Some of you probably wanted to prove to the world you'd recovered after the heartbreaking loss you suffered, but let's be honest... motivation coming from the outside rarely lasts. It's the inner voice that challenges you to continue improving every day, that fuels lasting success, lighting the fires, driving you to get better and better at what you do. It's the raging inferno in your soul that wakes you up in the middle of the night with an idea you can't wait to implement because it's the answer you were sure you'd never find. It's the whisper in the wind pushing you forward, continually reminding you failure is temporary and faithfully encouraging you to try again."

Israel was speechless. She'd described him so perfectly, it was like she'd read the words fate had written on his heart.

Fate never makes a mistake.

He wasn't sure where the words came from, but he understood their truth. Bristol was perfect for him. He just had to convince her, fate's timing was as flawless as its mating.

Chapter Six

AUSTIN LEANED AGAINST the nursery's doorframe, watching Charlotte nurse their son. He'd never seen anything more beautiful in his entire life. She took his breath away. Long, auburn waves of silk spilled over her shoulders, trailing well past her elbows. Her hair had grown so much while she was pregnant, he'd teased her about turning into Rapunzel. She'd assured him if she turned into a children's book character, it would be Mulan because there wasn't anything she wouldn't do for her family.

The reference hadn't meant anything to Austin, but a quick internet search promptly cleared up his confusion. The comparison was especially meaningful since she'd been trying to help her family and friends when she took the job as his assistant. Hell, he'd finally hired two people to replace her, and together, they didn't match her level of organization.

Charlotte offered to return to work, but Austin knew she wanted to stay home until Marshall started school. If she changed her mind, he would be thrilled to have her back in the office. Bending her over his desk and pushing himself balls deep into her slick heat would be the highlight of each workday. Looking down to see her rounded ass framed by a lace garter belt holding up silk stockings, his cock shuttling in and out, shining with her cream, would make work far more interesting. Who was he kidding? Adler Oil would sink like the Titanic because he'd never get anything done.

"I had to tune you out at *garter belt*. I was starting to feel flushed and needy... really needy."

"Little Star, you just gave birth. I can't imagine you feel up to what went through my mind." She gave an inelegant snort and had the audacity to roll her eyes. "You're running up a hell of a tab on swats, my love. That eye roll added a solid ten to the tally." His palm ached to connect with her bare ass, but the punishment would have to wait until he'd fucked them both into a coma.

It wasn't as if they hadn't had sex during her pregnancy. Hell, she'd been in a hormone-fueled sexual frenzy for months, but for the last several weeks, action had been scarce because he worried, she was doing too much. Hell, she'd overseen a major remodeling project, creating a nanny suite in addition to the nursery. He'd come home from work one night to find her asleep in the middle of the nursery floor, surrounded by animals she'd meticulously cut from a wallpaper mural. When he'd asked her why she was sleeping on the floor, her bright green eyes filled with tears.

"I couldn't get up. I'm a Weeble failure—I wobbled, but I couldn't get up."

Austin had almost bitten his tongue in two trying to keep from laughing. The whole scenario was funny until he found out how long she'd been stranded. She'd left her phone on the kitchen counter, so she had been unable to call anyone for help.

Austin heard a sniffle, the soft sound brought him back to the moment. He was horrified to see tears streaming down his mate's cheeks. *What the hell?* Pushing away from the doorframe, he across the room to kneel in front of the two most important people in the world.

"What's wrong, sweetheart? Talk to me."

"I want to be wanted again. I want to feel pretty. I'm tired of being a blimp. I already had the baby, and I'm still huge. I know I need to exercise, but I'm too tired. Why don't babies sleep longer than a couple of hours? And he eats all the time. My nipples hurt so bad, I'd go topless, but I'm terrified I might accidentally walk past a mirror. If it wasn't for Lindy, I'd have thrown myself off the damned balcony. I don't know how women do this... it's exhausting."

Fucking hell. How had he missed all these signs, despite every Dom he knew warning him about the baby blues? Sure, he knew the condition didn't typically start this soon, but with Charlotte's unique healing ability, it was no surprise she was well ahead of schedule.

The nanny they'd hired wasn't scheduled to arrive for a few days, so Cam Barnes suggested they hire Lindy Timish in the interim. Since she'd been at the reception, Lindy had already known Charlotte had given birth, and bless her heart, she'd been waiting for them when they arrived home. Stepping into the room, Lindy looked more like a recent high school graduate than a young woman studying for the bar exam. Austin grinned at her, wondering if any of the younger Doms at the club would ever brave Cam

Barnes wrath and claim the pretty brunette as their own. Everyone at the club knew she was under Cam's protection, and if that wasn't enough, Dr. Cecelia Barnes was standing right beside him. CeCe might be submissive to Cam, but she was hell on wheels when it came to her family and patients.

CeCe called Austin when she'd learned Lindy would be helping out until their nanny arrived. He joked later, the interrogation involved a hundred questions fired at him so quickly, his damned head was spinning by the time she'd finally been satisfied they weren't going to keep Lindy locked in a dungeon or planning to steal her away from their employ.

Lindy bounced into the room and grinned. "I saw the little bags of milk in the freezer. You're doing a great job with your pump. Y'all weren't kidding when you said Charlotte's body healed quickly. I know a lot of first-time mamas have trouble getting into the rhythm of nursing. Little man is set for the rest of the night and most of tomorrow, as well. Get some rest, Charlotte. Spend some time with your husband. Let him pamper you a little. You've earned it." Lindy lifted Marshall from Charlotte's arms, giving him a soft kiss on his forehead. Austin could have sworn the boy smiled—the little flirt. "Come on, handsome. Let's get you settled. My granny said babies grow when they're sleeping, so you better get to it. You have so many wonderful things to learn."

Lindy's voice trailed off as she moved down the hall. Cam and CeCe both stressed how much they appreciated the way she talked to their children. Lindy always said, "Babies are little people and deserve better than the nonsense-talk people subject them to. How are they supposed to grow up to be functioning adults if their brains are fed gibberish? It's insulting." Austin agreed and hoped the nanny they'd hired would be as forward-thinking as Lindy.

Austin looked at his wife, wondering how he was going to prove he wanted her just as much now as he had the first time he'd taken her to bed. When her image started to shimmer, he shook his head.

"Don't you dare disappear, Little Star. Your punishment swats are going to have to wait. I have something else in mind for tonight." He was flying by the seat of his pants. For the first time in years, he was going to walk into an evening with his sub and let her responses paint the scene without him leading.

Pulling Charlotte to her feet, he led her down the hall to the master suite. He'd have her naked and flat on her back in ten seconds flat if it were up to him, but, tonight, he wanted to touch her heart as well as her body. It was time for a little romance.

SPENDING THE DAY with Bristol had been enlightening and fun. Israel loved how her sharp mind functioned on multiple levels at the same time. Smiling to himself, he thought about how quickly she saw through any smokescreen he threw in her direction. At one point during lunch, she'd shaken her head and sighed.

"I don't understand it. I'm not usually this good at reading people. Most of the time, I'm borderline dim… or at the very least, I'm considered naïve when I'm dealing with anyone outside the office." She'd paused, watching him for any sign she was pushing too far before finally adding. "But with you... it seems like I know when you are trying to throw me off. I know shifters can speak telepathically while they are in their animal, but this feels different. I'm not sure how to put it into words."

Israel understood what she'd been unable to explain, but he didn't respond—some things are better left to the other person to sort through on their own. Any explanation he'd give her would fall short, so he decided it was best to simply redirect the conversation.

Dusk was settling outside the large window leading to his balcony. The glass railings and floor made it the perfect place to begin pushing the boundaries of the submissive side of Bristol's personality.

After spending the day talking with her, it hadn't come as a surprise when she admitted listing complete nudity as a hard limit at the club. He'd been pleased to learned Bristol had refused to have sex with any of the Doms she'd scened with. It was humbling to realize how pleased he was she hadn't been seriously involved with anyone at the club. Hell, from what he could tell, she wasn't getting much, period.

Opening the accordion-style glass doors to the patio, Israel crooked his finger, beckoning Bristol to join him. He'd given her another shirt to wear after her bubble bath that afternoon, and the thin white cotton did little to hide the outline of her areolas or the peaking of her nipples, anytime she noticed his appreciative gaze. A light breeze drifted around him, separating the front placket of the shirt, the two sides moving far enough apart to reveal her smooth mound. He shook his head when her hands moved to close the shirt. Bristol's hands fell to her sides, her face blushing his new favorite shade of scarlet. Her sex was lasered smooth, and the tantalizing glimpses revealed the outer folds of her labia were already glistening with arousal.

Gasping when she stepped out onto the balcony, Bristol forgot she was flashing anyone lucky enough to be looking up. When she settled her hands on the polished steel rail atop the glass panels, Israel moved close, caging her in by placing his hands on the rail, his arms framing her.

"Watching your expression as you take in the beauty surrounding us is like seeing it for the first time. Seeing the world through your eyes is a treat, baby." Pressing himself against her, he smiled to himself when he heard her soft gasp.

"I've never thought about how beautiful the downtown skyline would be. I'm living in a small second-floor apartment. I've paid off the student loans I had to take out to pay the living expenses my scholarships didn't cover. I've stayed in my little hovel, so I can save enough money to build my dream house. I already bought a large lot by the lake."

"Where is your lot?" He was surprised to learn she'd made a land purchase since it hadn't shown up in the background check.

"It's next to Cam and CeCe's. They bought several parcels through different holding companies to get around the purchase restrictions. It seems the covenants were written to keep people from buying up a huge chunk to insulate themselves. CeCe told me they weren't opposed to having neighbors, they were simply particular who they were." She looked over her shoulder and grinned, "I can feel your surprise. Don't worry, your report isn't inadequate. The sale was private. The contract and deed are being held by a bank until the last payment is made next month."

"You've built a successful medical practice, repaid your student loans, and paid off a tract of land. Beautiful, I don't think you need Bronx's advice." What she needed was a good business administrator to manage everything.

"You're right about the business manager, but they aren't easy to find."

Israel smiled to himself. Bristol answered as if he'd spoken aloud—their connection was growing and was particularly strong when they were touching. Putting his foot between hers, Israel pushed her right leg to the side, so her legs were shoulder-width apart.

"Keep your legs open, Beautiful. We're going to play a little. When I say *we're going to play*, you'll know it means we're in a scene. The dynamic between us changes from mates to Dominant and submissive. Tell me, you understand."

"I understand, Sir."

Fucking perfect.

"Perfect response, sweet sub." Unbuttoning the shirt, she'd chosen from his closet, Israel pulled the placket apart. Exposing her breasts to the cooler evening air, he rolled one nipple between his fingers, enjoying the way it tightened into a stiff peak. "I love how responsive you are. As a

Dom, there is nothing more satisfying. As your mate, it thrills me to know your body recognizes my desire."

Shifting his position, so his feet prevented her from moving hers back together, Israel wondered how long it would take her to notice the floor of his deck was glass as well as the sides. It was unlikely anyone would look up, and even if they did, only another shifter would have vision keen enough to see her exposed sex, but the feeling would still be the same. He didn't want to share her, but he loved doing public flogging scenes. A naked sub, tied and waiting for his lash, was heady indeed. Israel could hardly wait until they could perform at Prairie Winds.

There was something about the energy from an audience—it was always a powerful force added to a scene. Even nonmagicals benefitted from the powerful dynamic, but the effect was most noticeable with magicals. Shifters and other beings with special abilities were particularly sensitive to changes in electrical fields, so their excitement was fed by that of an enthusiastic audience. He hoped there was enough residual energy from the city below to give her a small taste of how sweet exhibitionism could be.

Bristol looked down, and Israel knew the moment she realized how exposed she was, despite the considerable distance to the ground. His gorgeous sub was suddenly struggling to cover what he considered his to show off.

"Don't move, Bristol," Israel growled. "You are precisely where I want you." She stopped moving, but he could feel the panic bubbling up inside her. "The only people who have a prayer of seeing you are other shifters, Beautiful. I am looking forward to showing you off. You are gorgeous. Lush, curvy, shining pink bits between the thighs of a real woman rather than a toothpick who spends all their time hungry—you are pure perfection. Stop believing what the magazines tell you is beautiful. Don't worry about what other people can see. Your Dom is the only one who counts, and right now, I want you to focus on the pleasure."

"Y-y-yes, Sir."

Israel looked forward to the day she'd recognize him as her master. He didn't want a 24/7 slave, but he'd be damned happy to know she saw him as the master of her pleasure.

"If I slid my hand between your legs, what would I find, Bristol? Are the folds of your pussy slick with your cream? I can smell your arousal—it's the sweetest fragrance on Earth." Sliding one hand slowly down her torso, Israel made certain he lingered over every curve. "Goddess above, you are a gift. Sexy curves, silky soft skin, and a brilliant mind. I'm more blessed than I deserve, but I'm not about to surrender a single godsend."

When he felt her tremble in his arms, he knew it wasn't because she was cold. Hell, heat was pouring off her. It was great to have a mate who was already a shifter. He understood exactly what her body signals meant and didn't need to worry about how her body would react to being claimed. She was close to climaxing, and his fingers were still several inches above paradise.

Bristol's faint whimper when he moved his hand from her breast was music to his ears. He was glad he'd had the foresight to wrap his arm around her, tightening his hold just beneath her breasts in case her knees folded out from under her, as he suspected they might. As an added bonus, her full breasts lifted in tempting invitation.

"You liked it when I pinched your nipples didn't you, Beautiful? I can hardly wait to experiment with clamps. Have you played with them before?"

"Yes. No." Israel smiled to himself—you have to love brilliant women. He'd asked two questions, and she'd answered both. Keeping his hands on her, he waited for more. He could feel her mind spinning and was more than willing to give her time to find the words she was searching for.

"I haven't played with much aside from a vibrator and light paddling. I spent most of my time observing when I was at the club. The other submissives kept telling me to let go and just have fun with it, but having sex with someone I didn't feel any connection with felt wrong."

He was grateful she'd followed her heart. He'd talked to enough subs over the years to know how devastating guilt could be when they caved to peer pressure. Knowing Bristol stayed true to herself meant they had one less challenge to overcome.

"The connection between us is so strong, and I know you can feel the electricity it generates. Hell, we'll probably set the place ablaze when we climax together. I want to give you a small sample of how great it will be. Lean your head back against my shoulder." He didn't want her falling forward. There was no way she could fall over the barrier, but she could damn well hit her head on the metal cap topping the glass wall. The satin curtain of her hair brushed against his cheek, making his cock swell to the point, he hoped there was enough blood pumping to his brain to keep him focused on Bristol's pleasure.

As soon as his fingers moved between her legs, she sagged against him. The rush of cream washing over his fingertips was pure liquid silk. Her folds were swollen, and he vowed to repeat this as a mini scene in front of a mirror, so he could see her labia flower open like the petals of a rose. The ancients described a woman's sex as a blood-red rose, and every Dom he knew agreed the comparison was spot on. Watching the petals of a woman's labia fill with blood and fold back like a blooming rose was one of life's most precious moments.

"There will be times, I want you to hold back your release, but that's another day... another scene. Not today and not now. Come when you are ready and as many times as you can." Using the calloused pad of his finger, Israel circled her clit until it was fully exposed.

"I'm so close... so, so... Oh. Yes." The words were airy and within seconds, lost in a scream of release he'd been looking forward to hearing. Israel loved hearing his mate shout his name as orgasm claimed her sanity for a brief moment in time. Feeling her collapse into his arms was as emotionally satisfying as it was sexually gratifying to feel her cream wash over his fingers.

"Again."

"I can't. I've never been able to..." He tightened his hold, interrupting her denial.

"You can. You will. Give it to me, Beautiful." Slipping his fingers into her soaked vagina, Israel felt her stiffen against him. "Don't you dare be embarrassed by that magnificent sound. Damn, that's a huge turn on. Knowing you are so wet, we can hear the sound above the traffic is hotter than hell." Curving his fingers, the tips brushed against the soft spongy spot that sent her into orbit. Two more orgasms, one immediately on the heels of the first, left her limp in his arms. He sucked her juices from his fingers, savoring the tangy flavor of the woman destined to be his mate.

Picking her up, Israel simply held her for several long seconds, loving the way she felt cradled in his arms. Rolling Bristol into his chest, he relished her soft moan when he nuzzled his nose in her hair. He looked forward to claiming her as his mate, but for now, he would have to be satisfied with a killer round of *swinging from the chandeliers* sex.

Claiming Bristol was his goal, but he'd count *knock you on your ass* sex as a close second. He'd already ordered their dinner, but it wasn't scheduled to be delivered for another two hours. Yes, indeed, he had plenty of time to make love to the woman whose orgasms lit up downtown Austin a couple minutes ago. Hearing her cries of pleasure fill the evening air was humbling and notched up his desire for her more than ever.

Looking down at her, spread out on his bed, Israel couldn't get out of his clothes fast enough. He had a condom rolled on and was moving over her within seconds. Skimming his lips over the shell of her ear, he appreciated the goosebumps racing over the surface of her skin. Her nipples were tight peaks pressing against his chest, and the heat of her sex was teasing the tip of his cock.

"I want you, Bristol. I want to make sweet, achingly slow love to you, but I think I'm past that point. This is going to be hard and fast—we'll get to slow and sweet in a few minutes." Her body answered for her. The scent of her honey floated around him as she lifted her legs, opening herself even more—until no part of her sex was hidden from his view. The head of his cock pushed through the outer folds, the heat so intense, he fought back the urge to plunge in balls deep. "You're so tight... so hot. Goddess above, you feel like heaven."

The muscles of her vagina were rippling around him, the rhythmic contractions trying to pull him deeper. He could hardly wait to fuck her without anything between them. They hadn't talked about it yet, and he hadn't wanted to take time for that conversation tonight. This evening was about establishing a deeper level of trust required for a solid foundation of intimacy. Relationships between shifters typically moved much faster than non-shifters, in large part, because they were such sexual creatures. Israel knew it was important to stay tuned in to Bristol's verbal and nonverbal messages, but it was getting more and more difficult.

"Please. I want to feel you all the way inside me. Your cock is hot. And huge." *Holy hell, please go slow. It's been so long.*

He wasn't sure how long it had been, but she was so tight, he knew he needed to take a deep breath and focus on inching forward. Tuning in to Bristol's needs was a mixed blessing. Her body was clamoring for patience, but her soul longed for something more demanding—the hard-core, pounding into the mattress sex he longed to give her.

Chapter Seven

BRISTOL'S MIND WAS melting from pleasure. The heat coming from Israel was so intense, she was having trouble keeping her thoughts from evaporating into a fine mist. Everything about the man was hot, and when he came over her, resting most of his weight on his forearms, there was still enough pressure, she had no doubt who was in charge. He'd said tonight was all about her pleasure, and she understood what he was trying to do, but the truth was, her pleasure fed off his. She needed to feel wanted. Feeling desirable was gas to her flame, and he was pouring it on by the gallon.

The rounded head of his cock was sliding through her slick folds, and the anticipation was killing her. Bristol hadn't had sex in so long, she'd started referring to herself as a born-again virgin. The other subs at the club laughed, but there was a sad element of truth, Bristol found embarrassing. She'd spent years learning how to bring babies into the world and often wondered if she would have any of her own. Hell, the way her love life had been the past few years, immaculate conception was her only hope. *I keep watching for that damned star... but so far, nada.*

"Bristol, I would like nothing more than to make your

love life the envy of every woman you know. When you are mine, I'll make certain you're well satisfied, and I'll look forward to the time you're ready to start a family." She could hear the sincerity in his voice, and if she wasn't careful, he was going to slip right past every last one of her defenses.

Damn, why did fate send me the right man at the wrong time?

"Have faith, Beautiful. Fate never makes mistakes. Now, I want to refocus on enjoying the feel of your soft curves. Damn, you feel so fucking amazing. I'm going to map every square inch of your luscious body with my tongue. I'll know each sweet spot—what makes you moan, what elicits a gasp, what makes you blush, and what triggers those hot little goosebumps I saw earlier."

His words distracted her from the shallow thrusts he was using to give her body time to adjust to the intrusion. The heat generated by her stretching tissues felt like flames licking up and down her vagina, wrapping him in heat so intense, she hoped it was scorching his control. She wanted him to shove himself in until his scrotum slapped against her ass, but she worried the move could actually tear her in places she'd rather not have stitched up. She'd seen the damage that could be done, and it wasn't pretty.

But I want him buried deep inside. Now.

"We're so close, Beautiful. I won't ordinarily allow your mind to wander while I'm fucking you, but tonight it served my purpose."

"Something... oh, dear Goddess... to remember."

"Indeed. I want you to stay in the moment. The only mental field trip I'll allow is subspace, and I'll be happy to have you launch into that part of your head anytime you can manage it." Her vaginal muscles rippled around him, and he smiled down at her. "Have you ever been in subspace, my sweet mate?

"No. I'm not sure I'll be able to let go enough for it to happen." She'd heard subs talk about the joys of the endorphin-induced high, but she'd never come close to experiencing it. She'd never thought it would be possible, but she hadn't thought she could have one orgasm immediately after another, either.

"Trust me to take you where you need to go, Sweetheart. I'll get you where you need to be. You only need to put yourself in my care." He didn't give her time to protest before pulling back, leaving only the head of his long cock sheathed before he jerked his hips forward. The heated tip pushed against her cervix, and Bristol heard herself scream as pure, white-hot pleasure streaked through her body.

"Yes. Again. Oh, please don't stop. It's so hot... so good... More. Now." Bristol didn't know if she was speaking the words aloud or if they were only being shouted in her mind. A small part of her knew it wouldn't matter, Israel would hear them either way. The slow pace he set felt good, but she wanted more. She *needed* more. Maybe... if she could shift her position...

"Stay where I put you, little sub. When I want you to lift your glorious ass, I'll tell you." Israel's pace never changed, but his voice was pure sexual dominance. "Who is in charge of your pleasure, Beautiful?"

"You, Sir. You're in charge." Bristol finally understood the needy tone she so often heard in other submissives' voices during scenes. The begging tone often came off as manipulative whining, but now, it felt more sincere. Holy handmaidens, she wouldn't have been able to speak in a normal tone if her life depended on it.

"Talk to me, mate. Tell me what you need. I may be able to hear your thoughts, but the heat we're generating creates static, making telepathy unreliable, at best. I want to feel your pussy milking my cock the way it did my fingers. The liquid rush of your release coating my fingers was one of the most erotic things I've ever experienced, and I already know feeling it coat my dick is going to blow my mind."

Bristol could feel her body slipping deeper into arousal, the pressure in her womb winding tighter and tighter. It was only a matter of seconds until the spring inside her sex snapped... Damn, she hoped her brain cells didn't fry. There was a very real chance she was going to be left a mumbling shell of herself.

"Harder... please... Sir." Surprise whispered through her mind. She wasn't sure how she'd managed to push the words out, but his response was immediate—and perfect.

"My pleasure, little sub." Israel's voice was laced with satisfaction and tenderness, but his body's response was the polar opposite. The muscles of his back were sheets of steel beneath his sweat-dampened skin.

Bristol could feel the subtle increase in tension as his hips thrust harder and faster. Once... twice... The third time their bodies met, hers erupted in a blinding release. A keening wail in the distance registered in the back of her mind, but whoever the woman was, she was on her own. Bristol was too caught up in her own glitter storm to worry about someone else. Bright, sparkling lights behind her eyelids burst into colors so brilliant, they defied description.

"Open your eyes, Bristol. Now. I want to see into your soul when you come." Her eyes opened on their own, and she was astonished how quickly the muscles responded to his command. "Your body recognizes its mate and Master, Bristol. Let go. I'll catch you."

His reassurance was the last thing she heard before a second orgasm hit her with even more force than the first. Bristol felt her back arch involuntarily, a millisecond before everything around her disappeared in a blinding flash of white, sending her tumbling into darkness.

ISRAEL WAS WRAPPED in the most intense heat he'd ever experienced. He'd been sexually active since he was a teen and never experienced anything close to the mind-melting release he'd just had with Bristol. Reading about the deeper connection hadn't done anything to prepare him for the reality. Mustering the last vestiges of his strength, Israel rolled to the side without pulling out of his mate. It didn't matter he hadn't officially claimed her—Bristol Banks belonged to him.

A brief flash of a woman's face moved through his mind so fast, it didn't register, but a spike of fear followed so close behind, he knew they connected. His thinking was so fogged by all the happy chemicals free-floating in his brain, Israel wasn't sure he'd be able to fight his way out of a wet paper bag. Whoever she was, she needed to tread carefully. Threatening Bristol wouldn't be tolerated—ever. The Adlers hadn't become a force to be reckoned with by rolling over and playing dead.

"Wow." Bristol started to stir against him, but he tightened the arm he'd slung over her back.

"Stay where you are, Beautiful." He wanted to give their heartbeats a chance to synchronize. The fastest way he knew to deepen their connection was to let their hearts beat as one. A deeper link between them would bring her around faster—preventing physical distance was easy, stopping her emotional retreat was much more difficult.

"Why did you think about Clovia Wilson?" Without the enhanced hearing of a shifter, Israel wouldn't have been able to hear her whispered question. It wasn't so much the query he hated as the defeated tone and raw pain he could hear in her voice.

"I saw a flash of a face, but it was gone before I could make it out. Who is she?" The name sounded vaguely familiar, but his brain wasn't fully online yet, so he hadn't been able to figure out why the name would mean anything to him.

"She's a nurse in the OB ward at the hospital and a shifter. I've heard she is a member of the club, but I've never seen her there."

"Wait, let me check something." Israel picked his phone up from the nightstand and checked his messages. Turning the phone to her, Israel showed Bristol the message he got hours earlier from Austin. "I'm not as worried about this message as I am the one from Bronx." Turning the phone back to her, he felt her tense as she read the text.

There was a woman standing outside the front entrance who said she's your mate. Sorry, bro, but don't think that sailor has both her oars in the water. My crazy meter pinged off the chart. You better pull up the security feed and check her out.

When Bristol struggled to move, Israel let her go, but he wasn't going to allow her out of his reach. Bristol turned to the master bath, intent on retreating, but he captured her wrist. Giving her a quick tug, so she was standing between his splayed knees, he brushed the backs of his knuckles over her lower jaw. Her knees barely touching his erection, and he was pleased when her eyes drifted closed, a pink tinge staining her cheeks.

"Yes, I want you again, but you won't be able to concentrate until we get to the bottom of this. I'd feel the same if our positions were reversed." He gave her a reassuring smile but wasn't convinced she bought it. "I'll bring you something to wear. When you're ready, come to my home office. I can access the outside security footage from my laptop." She gave him a quick nod but refused to meet his gaze. When she tried to move away, he held tight.

"No, Beautiful. That isn't how this is going to go." She didn't respond for several seconds but finally lifted her face to his. Worse than the pain he'd heard in her voice was the self-recrimination he saw in her eyes. *Fucking hell.*

"I'd like to get dressed and head home. You are more than capable of sorting this out without my help. I'm already embarrassed enough. Good heavens, I had sex with a coworker's boyfriend."

Israel was shocked. Did she really believe his moral character was that despicable? Fuck, he wanted to pull her over his lap and paddle her until she understood how wrong she was, but that wouldn't help him build the relationship he was striving for.

"No, Sweetheart. I want you right beside me while I figure out what's going on. I have not been in a committed relationship for several years, and even then, I knew she wasn't my mate. We both knew it was a temporary convenience and remained friends after it ended." Now that his head had cleared, Israel was convinced he knew who he was dealing with, but he wasn't going to say anything to Bristol until he was sure. "You don't know me well enough to know I'd never cheat on my mate—I understand that it takes time—but I assure you, I was raised to have more integrity." Moving to the dresser, he picked up her phone and dialed.

"Who are you calling?"

"Prairie Winds." She looked surprised but didn't say anything. "You trust Kent and Kyle West, right?" Submissives seemed to naturally gravitate to the two club owners. Both male and female submissives respected the Club Masters, instinctively trusting the pair to keep them safe. Israel knew Kyle and Kent considered all the club's members as their responsibility, but they made it clear to everyone, the subs were under their personal protection.

"Yes, I trust them. Their screening process was so intrusive, it was actually reassuring. I also respect them. I've never seen them look at any submissive the way they look at Tobi. Every submissive I know admires them. They are always willing to listen, and I don't think the club would be the same without their guidance. I've heard subs describe them as their best friend's big brothers. You can talk to them about anything."

He'd heard other submissives at the club make the same observation. Israel was happy she'd had someone at the club she trusted. He belonged to clubs all over the country and could say with complete confidence, safety was the make-or-break element for a successful kink club. The best way to ensure safety was good training and mentoring programs.

Pushing the last number, he wasn't surprised to hear Kyle's concerned greeting.

"Bristol, are you alright? Are you in a safe place?"

"Bristol is fine, my friend. This is Israel. She's with me at Adler Oil. We've had an issue come up, but I'll explain more later. I'd like you to answer any question she asks you about me with complete honesty. It's important she knows who she's dealing with. I'm handing her the phone, then leaving the room." Israel put the phone in Bristol's hand, kissed her on the forehead, and walked away.

Chapter Eight

C LOVIA PACED THE length of her luxury apartment's balcony, barely resisting the urge to throw her damned patio furniture over the edge. Watching it shatter on the sidewalk wouldn't be near as satisfying as heaving it across the street. After Israel's brother refused to help her enter Adler Oil, she'd been confronted by a member of the building's security team. Had he really thought she was going to hand over her identification? Not fucking likely.

She was growing tired of waiting for Israel to figure out they were fated to be together. She'd known immediately when she'd seen him, but after they shared a scene, Clovia was shocked he hadn't felt the connection. During after-care, he'd been polite but distant, leaving her as though his mind was somewhere else. She'd been relieved when she heard his sister had been in some kind of danger. Clovia didn't give a rat's ass about his sister but was damned happy to find out why her mate had been so distracted.

Clovia knew how lucky she'd been to find a luxury apartment directly across the street from the building where her future mate lived. When she'd realized the apartment's balcony faced Israel's, she'd willingly agreed to the seller's outrageous asking price. Tapping into her trust fund was a paperwork nightmare, but it had been worth the effort. Walking back to her building after picking up dinner, Clovia heard a woman's scream of passion.

Enhanced hearing meant she could make out nuances of sound others missed and heard things they couldn't—the limitation was being able to determine where the sound came from. It took her a few seconds to zero in on Israel's suite since she hadn't been expecting him to take Dr. B home with him. All the subs at Prairie Winds knew Master Israel only played at the club. She overheard them discussing him on several occasions, and the small group of women seemed amazed he never took a sub home for a night or weekend of play.

Clovia moved back inside, stepping behind the section of her glass doors with the privacy screening. The high definition telescope she bought was perfect for looking into Israel's windows, and the addition of the screen meant she could see out, but no one knew she was watching them.

"Seriously, people need to learn to close their damned curtains if they are going to have sex with their neighbor in their living room."

Hell, she'd taken enough pictures to net a fortune. A banker and his physician wife living in the building next to Adler Oil, both paid her for the pictures she'd taken of them fucking other people.

Focusing on the windows directly across from hers, Clovia wondered where the two had gone. They were no longer on the balcony, and she didn't see lights in any of the other rooms. Israel rarely closed the curtains, and she'd enjoyed watching him moving around nude in the moderately sized space. *You have to love shifters and their lack of inhibitions regarding nudity.*

Clovia was a wolf shifter who'd been raised in a household of mountain lion shifters. She never fit in and often struggled with the finer points of her special abilities. She enjoyed running free in the open spaces of her family's large ranch but learned the hard way, not everyone appreciated her animal form. After her adoptive parents died, attorneys had quickly sold off the assets and set up her trust fund.

Clovia was only nineteen years old when she found herself standing on the sidewalk in front of the law office, holding the key to a modest apartment across the street from the college where she was attending nursing school. The grisly old fart handed her a checkbook, a hundred dollars cash, and told her he'd make sure her rent was paid until she was gainfully employed. It had taken some legal maneuvering, but she'd gotten control of the money earlier than anyone expected. She surprised the court when she'd invested most of the trust, only leaving a small portion of the sizeable fortune liquid.

The only large purchase she'd made was the condo. She'd been tracking the local real estate market and knew the property was appreciating. Once she and Israel were mated, she planned to sell her place and reinvest in a larger home out by the lake, where they could enjoy running in the woods. Clovia had her eye on a piece of real estate next to Master Cam's, but no one seemed to know who owned it. She didn't intend to give up until she owned the lot located adjacent to Cam and CeCe Barnes. It was close to Prairie Winds, so she and Israel would be able to utilize the club as often as they wanted.

If she wasn't scheduled to work in a couple of hours, Clovia would have happily poured herself a large glass of wine and settled back with her telescope. She needed to replenish her photo supply—after all, why should she use her own money when her neighbors were so willing to pay her for pictures, they didn't want the world to see? A few of them had gotten smart, pulling the curtains before entertaining guests, their spouses or significant others didn't know about, but several believed they paid for protection in advance. They hadn't.

Clovia considered her nursing career a temporary inconvenience. She'd planned to find a wealthy, well-established doctor to marry—unconcerned about his appearance or marital status, as long as he was rich—but meeting her mate changed everything. Israel Adler was a sexual Dominant, a shifter, owned his own security company, and fucking loaded—in short, he was perfect, and he was hers. Bristol Banks didn't know who she was up against. Clovia had no intention of losing her mate to a woman who lived in a tiny studio apartment and drove a car older than her embarrassing wardrobe. *Honestly, it looks like the woman shops at third-rate thrift shops. What the hell is she doing with her money?*

Moving to her bedroom, Clovia stripped out of her clothing, washed her face, slathered on moisturizer, and went to bed. Her upcoming shift at the hospital would be interesting—she was scheduled to work with Dr. B. Clovia vowed to stay close to her... maybe she'd be willing to talk about what happened after Israel Adler carried her to his car. The good doctor wasn't known for sharing information about her personal life, but perhaps she only needed a little prompting.

BRISTOL MOVED TO sit in the chair facing Israel's desk, but his frown stopped her before she could lower herself onto the soft leather seat. When she didn't move, he shook his head before turning in his own seat and holding out his hand to her.

"Come here, Beautiful." Her bare feet moved silently around the desk without her mind registering the movement.

"Thank you, Sweetheart. Did Kyle answer your questions?" Kyle texted Israel when he finished the call, assuring him everything had gone well but hadn't gone into detail about their conversation.

"I didn't really need to ask any questions. I apologize for insulting your character... that wasn't my intention. I was reeling from the news another woman considers you her mate." Her fingers were laced together so tightly, they were turning white. Bristol's hands were small enough, he easily wrapped them both in his much larger one.

"We won't always agree about everything, but there are a few things I can promise you without hesitation. Your safety and happiness will always be my number one priority, and I will never give you any reason to doubt my faithfulness—simply put, I'll never cheat on you." He gave her what his mom always called his boyish grin and added, "I won't promise to never lie because birthdays, Christmas, and special surprises often require certain levels of deception."

Bristol's posture relaxed, and Israel was relieved his reassurance had been on point. Time to move on.

"I want you to look at some of the security footage from the outside the building. My brother, Bronx, encountered a woman, trying to get into the building. She told him she was my mate, a claim he already knew was false, so he refused to allow her inside. He tipped off the security team, then alerted me. When the night staff confronted her, she refused to give her name and swore she didn't have any identification on her. Since it isn't illegal to stand on the sidewalk, my men had no reason to hold her or to alert law enforcement." He brought up the footage, beginning with the woman walking up the street several minutes before Bronx entered the frame.

"Clovia Williams."

Israel's vision went red for a split second, and he felt a growl rumble deep in his chest. He took a deep breath, making a concentrated effort to calm his anger.

"If she is claiming she's your mate, why didn't your brother believe her? How does he know it's not true?"

What the fuck? When I find out who betrayed her trust, I'll rip them to shreds.

"I'm sure Bronx heard that I met you at the reception. My brothers and sisters know I've been looking forward to meeting my mate, so word would have spread like wildfire. We are each other's biggest cheerleaders and harshest critics, and none of us are swayed by the notoriety of any member of our family." Her soft laughter was exactly the reaction he'd been hoping for. She was going to need a sense of humor to deal with the direction their conversation was heading.

"I work with Clovia, but I don't know her well. I'm usually dealing with families or trying to wade through mountains of paperwork when the nurses are visiting. It isn't that I'm trying to be a snob, though it probably seems that way."

Re-reading Bristol's file while he'd waited for her at the hospital had been enlightening, but listening to the nurses chattering down the hall had been even more so. As non-shifters, they never considered the possibility he could hear them. Most of the small group's gossip centered around their plans for the next weekend—evidently, there was a hospital-sponsored picnic at the lake, no one wanted to miss. Some had already made plans while others were waiting to find out if they could find someone to cover for them.

Only once had the conversation turned to one of their co-workers. Several expressed concern about Dr. B's exhaustion, wondering if it was safe for her to drive. He vowed to find out which of the nurses said she planned to drive Bristol home. The young woman was going to find herself on the receiving end of a hefty bonus.

The others reminded Nurse Considerate she was risking being fired for leaving the hospital before her shift was over, but she'd remained committed to making certain Bristol got home safely. He'd moved to the nurses' station, hoping to identify the sweetheart among them, but his sudden appearance silenced their conversation.

"I'm waiting to drive Dr. Banks home. Can you tell me how much longer she'll be?"

Before her co-workers could respond, he saw her walking down the hall. Bristol hadn't seen him, but he'd known two things. One, she was only a couple of minutes from tumbling ass over tea kettle into an exhaustion-induced meltdown, and two, she'd fight to her last breath to hold it together when she saw him. Damn it, he had five sisters and knew how they rallied if they thought a man they were interested in was watching. Bristol Banks was every bit as strong and stubborn as his sisters, and the minute her eyes met his, he knew he'd called it right.

Returning his attention to the curvy armful sitting on his lap, Israel moved his hand in slow circles over her lower back, hoping she found the contact as soothing as he did. Listening as her mind tried to sort through the previous two days events, one word popped up time and again. *Coffee*. He chuckled, setting her on her feet.

"Come. Let's get you caffeinated, so you'll be able to focus. I don't usually drink coffee, so I often forget others do—much to my family's disdain. It seems I'm the odd-man-out when it comes to the *elixir of the gods*, as Asia refers to it." The suite he'd chosen wasn't large, but he'd remodeled the kitchen before moving in.

"Holy Martha Stewart. This kitchen is bigger than my entire apartment." When he arched a brow in her direction, she read his doubt and nodded. "I'm not kidding when I refer to my hovel as small. It's a studio apartment in a run-down building. I work a lot, so it doesn't matter." Israel wanted to laugh at her last comment, suspecting she used the simple explanation often.

"This kitchen is amazing, but it would be wasted on me. Cooking doesn't seem to be in my skill set. One of my college professors tried to relate her upper-level pharmacology course to cooking, and I almost failed the damned class." She rolled her eyes in exasperation, "I still think comparing cooking to chemistry is a staggering overestimation. Assuming people know the names of a zillion different ingredients is presumptuous. Why, in the name of all things holy, do they use so many foreign words to describe things? Some are Italian, some are French... the list is endless."

Israel leaned his head back and laughed. Her mini-rant told him far more about her than the words alone. He was pleased she felt safe enough with him to be herself. Brilliant, beautiful, and a sense of humor? Fate had been good to him.

"I understand your frustration with the terminology since most medical terms are so easily understood." He added a nod to the mocking comment, but she wasn't going for it.

"Was that sarcasm? It sure sounded like sarcasm. What happens to your subs if they cop an attitude? I bet you punish them for being flip." Israel was in front of her before she could pull in a deep breath, his fingers capturing her chin, tilting her face up, so they were face to face.

"It was teasing. Outside a scene, I will take as good as I give, but you've pushed yourself into dangerous territory. My real issue with your comment is the allusion to other subs. Rest assured, my lovely mate, from the moment your scent drifted to me, every other submissive faded from my memory. As a shifter, you should be well aware of how this works, so your comment represents a deliberate challenge." He kissed her forehead, letting his lips linger, brushing the surface of her skin with a touch meant to comfort. "Challenges... every challenge will be answered."

I knew it was too good to be true. Why do I always say the wrong thing? Get through this and go home. Go to work and stick to what you know.

Israel was astonished. Did she really believe he'd walk away from her because she'd challenged him? He wanted to kick the ass of whoever convinced this amazing woman she had to be perfect all the time. The physical toll associated with that level of pressure had to be suffocating, and the emotional burden would be enough to break the strongest person. Pulling her into his arms, Israel held her close until he felt her relax.

"When was the last time you had more than a day off?" He felt her stiffen, but he wasn't going to back down. Their future depended on them being able to speak openly about everything, even if it was out of her comfort zone.

"You mean like a vacation?"

He already knew the answer, the tone of her voice giving her away. Bristol's response had been something between disbelief and worry. Did she think he was going to judge her for doing what she loved?

"No, I mean more than two consecutive days."

"There isn't any reason for me to take off." Her eyes focused on something over his left shoulder.

He didn't ordinarily allow subs to hide, but in this case, he sensed she needed a little distance to pull her thoughts together. Bristol had been on her own for a long time—having a mate was going to be a big adjustment for her. Israel nodded for her to continue, watching her take a deep breath, then another before speaking. This time, her words were so subdued, they had an air of defeat.

"I don't have a family to visit. It seems unfair for me to

take off and sit in my apartment while my co-workers miss their family celebrations."

He understood what she was saying. He'd had employees in similar positions, and there had been one common thread—they'd all suffered burn-out. After one quit, Israel started insisting the other two took their vacations and stayed in the rotation to have holidays off. They'd grumbled but thanked him later. He was considering how to best convince her she needed to dial it back when his phone rang. Since he'd set it to only accept emergency calls, he sighed and reached for the annoying device.

After talking to Austin and Bronx earlier in the day, Israel had worried Clovia might be mentally unstable, but he didn't have any evidence she was dangerous. Gut feelings aside, he didn't have anything to indicate Bristol wouldn't be safe at the hospital. Before he could ask his mate any more about her upcoming shift, his phone chirped with an incoming message. This time the text was from Parker Andrews, the Chief of Police. Frowning, Israel turned the screen so Bristol could read the message.

We are looking for Dr. Bristol Banks. Her apartment was broken into an hour ago.

Chapter Nine

B RISTOL READ THE message twice before the words made sense. Her initial reaction was disbelief and shock, followed quickly by anger, then amusement. When she realized Israel had gone perfectly still beneath her, Bristol took a deep breath before turning to face him.

"I guess I'd better get dressed. Please let him know I will be there as soon as I catch a cab." She tried to get to her feet, but he held tight. Looking up to meet his gaze, Bristol smiled. "I'll be okay, it was just a bit of a surprise. Anyone desperate enough to break into my place needs the clothes worse than I do. I don't keep much in my apartment because there isn't much space there." He studied her for long seconds before setting her on her feet.

"Let's go." The rough tone of his voice made it clear it was pointless to argue.

If she was honest with herself, Bristol was relieved she wouldn't have to face the situation alone. No doubt, she would be forced to field questions, she wouldn't know the answer to and be subjected to the questioning looks of officials who wouldn't understand why she was willing to live in such a pathetic dump. Someone who'd never been poor might not understand why she felt the need to save every cent she could.

"My sisters have clothes in the closet of the spare bedroom. Help yourself to anything you need. I'm going to make a few calls while I wait for you."

The independent woman inside her wanted to tell him she was more than capable of handling this on her own, but an impending sense of danger kept her from speaking up.

"Thank you. I... well, I appreciate you offering to take me. I'm not sure how the police knew to contact you, but I'm always surprised how connected people are here in Austin." Bristol had always felt isolated, forced to deal with grown-up challenges early, forging her independent nature, but it also meant she hadn't spent any time networking—a skill the members of Prairie Winds seemed to have refined to a science.

An hour later, Bristol stood in the middle of her small apartment, staring in resigned disbelief at the tattered remnants of her personal belongings. The few dishes she'd accumulated over the years lay broken on the floor. Judging by their positions and the dents in the cheap sheetrock, she assumed they'd been thrown at the walls with considerable force. Every piece of clothing had been shredded, the tattered garments piled on the floor nearly unrecognizable.

"Can you tell if anything is missing, Dr. Banks?" The man Israel introduced as Parker Andrews, the local police chief, was looking at her with concern. She'd seen him at Prairie Winds but hadn't known his name or what he did for a living until today.

"Honestly, I don't think so. I didn't have much. My

laptop is at the office, and my tablet is in my bag. Diplomas and things like that are kept at the office. I didn't have any jewelry other than what you see." Waving her hand around the room where a few things she'd picked up over the years lay broken on the floor, Bristol took a deep breath, trying to hold back the sudden wave of emotion washing over her.

No one had said it out loud, but she wasn't naïve. This was an act of rage rather than a burglary. The realization she'd made an enemy, capable of an act this senseless was humbling and terrifying at the same time. How was she going to get this mess cleaned up before her shift started in a few hours?

Bristol knew she could hire a cleaning crew, but it seemed like a waste of time and money since there wasn't anything left worth saving. All she needed was a scoop shovel and a bunch of trash bags. Thank the heavens, she didn't keep anything of value here. Hell, the entire complex was a crime waiting to happen. She was surprised this wasn't a weekly event. Taking a deep breath and straightening her spine, Bristol wasn't going to wallow in self-pity. It was just stuff and certainly not anything she couldn't replace over time. Looking up, she was surprised to see Chief Andrews looking at her thoughtfully, his gaze intent and assessing.

"Do you have any idea who might want to hurt you, Dr. Banks?"

"No, I'm baffled. I don't have any enemies that I'm aware of. This isn't the best neighborhood, as I'm sure you already know." She wanted to believe it was a random act, but something about it felt personal. Looking up to meet his gaze, she tried to smile. "Please… call me, Bristol."

Bristol appreciated Israel stepping aside, so she could field questions without interference. He'd stood at the side of the room, his quiet presence a balm to her rattled spirit. She could feel his unwavering support, wondering what it was like growing up in a family where people looked out for one another.

Shaking her head, she looked down, toeing some of the perfume-soaked fabric away from her shoes.

"Wait. The perfume… it's not mine." *Why would someone bring their own perfume to destroy my apartment?* Bristol felt herself sway as a sense of dread moved through her.

You smell like a wet dog. How can you stand yourself? Go sleep outside. No, we'll still smell you on the back porch. I don't care if it's fucking snowing, you stink, and we've got people coming over.

A chill moved through her as a flashback played so vividly in her mind, she nearly fell to her knees and begged to be allowed to stay inside. Her parents hadn't been shifters, and they'd never stopped cursing fate for saddling them with a *demon child*. Their abuse had taken many forms, but it was their emotional distance that hurt the most.

"Come back to me, Beautiful." Blinking, Bristol brought Israel's handsome face into focus. His expression was grim but filled with compassion rather than sympathy. "Good girl. Stay with us, Sweetheart." She followed his line of sight when he glanced to the side, surprised to see his brother, Bronx, standing nearby. Flashing her a smile, she was sure had women falling at his feet, Bristol felt herself smile. *Hell, I bet he was as charming as he was incorrigible as a child.*

"Incorrigible doesn't even begin to cover it, Beautiful." Israel kissed her forehead, then turned her to his brother. "Let Bronx walk you down to the car. He'll be happy to show you whatever pimp-mobile he's driving."

"Hey, I'll have you know a McLaren 720S is not a pimp-mobile—it's designed to impress a future sister-in-law. Who knows, I might even convince her she's making a terrible mistake hooking up with you." When he wrapped a protective arm around her shoulders to escort her out of her trashed apartment, Bristol was relieved to feel nothing but protective, brotherly energy surround her. The man was obviously a world-class flirt, but it was equally apparent that's where it ended.

"Get your own woman." Israel's barked response was followed by a much softer warning. *Take care of her, Bronx. I'm entrusting you with the most important person in the world.* Bristol might have thought those words were the end of the telepathic communication if she'd heard Bronx respond. Once they were seated in Bronx's car, she turned to him and raised her brow in question, and he laughed.

"Yes, there was more, but it was about what he would do to me if anything happened to you. Very tacky. You could do better, you know."

She found herself relaxing, despite the mess she'd just left. The supple leather seats cocooned her, the sound system made it seem as though they'd gotten front row seats at a Kenny Chesney concert, and the new car smell made her forget the obnoxious smell of the perfume in her apartment. When Bronx started the car, she turned and started to speak, but he shook his head.

"Israel wants to do this for you, Bristol. My brother

takes care of all of us. He drops everything and flies all over the country when one of us is in trouble, yet never asks for anything. Honestly, I can't remember the last time he asked anyone to lend a hand, so when he asked me to take you shopping, I agreed without a second thought."

"Shopping? Why would he want you to take me shopping?"

"Sister, your clothes are shredded, and even if they weren't, the stench would be enough reason to send them all to the dumpster. We can replace stuff, but it will take a while longer to get that damned smell out of my nose. Freaking hell, that was nasty."

She couldn't argue with his comments about the perfume. The disgusting scent had no doubt been chosen explicitly because it was overpowering and gross and easily covered the scent of whoever had been in her apartment.

"You don't have to take me shopping, Bronx. I have a few things at my office, and I'm sure you have plenty of other things you'd rather be doing."

"A *few* things? Okay, listen. If I don't take you, my sisters are going to swarm you like a hive of bees. You'll be stuck hitting every high-end store in Austin before they decide there isn't enough locally for you to choose from, then you'll find yourself spirited off to Dallas before you know what hit you." Shaking his head, Bronx grinned, "You'll be traumatized for life, and Israel will be pissed because I didn't follow instructions. To be perfectly honest, I don't want to disappoint him when he never asks for anything—and of course, there's the fact, he's a pain in the ass when he's mad."

She didn't know any of the Adlers well, but she was

coming to realize they were usually teasing when they sounded the most serious. The unrepentant grin lighting up Bronx's handsome face was all the confirmation she needed.

"Israel warned me you tend to take things literally, so I'll try to curb my sarcasm. Probably wouldn't be a good idea to place any large bets on my success." Shaking his head as they turned onto the highway leading to the city's high-end shopping district, he flashed her another well-practiced charming smile. "Shopping sucks and having to scale back the snark is going to be a challenge, but on the flip side, we get to spend a chunk of Israel's money. Top that off with the bragging rights, I'll get with the girls, and we have a winner."

"He can't buy me clothes… it's too much. It doesn't matter, anyway. I have to be at the hospital in a couple of hours, so I don't have time for this foray into retail hell. I need to get my car moved to…" Damn, where was she going to stay until her apartment was fixed?

"Parker already called the hospital." Bristol felt her mouth drop open and her blood pressure spike. "Oh, shit, I know that look. Any man who survives childhood with five sisters recognizes that expression. Chill, little sister. The chief doesn't want you hurt on his watch—he's just doing his job. How would it look if he didn't protect the city's favorite doctor? You think he wants to answer to all those pissed-off pregnant women or their husbands?"

She could only stare at him, shocked speechless.

"Yeah, didn't think so, and this isn't even mentioning that he's a Dom. You see where this is headed, right?"

Bristol let out a breath she didn't realize she'd been

holding and nodded. The hospital was fairly secure against outsiders, but she'd be a sitting duck if Clovia Williams was the culprit, and Bristol's gut instinct told her the woman who considered Israel hers was a couple of sandwiches short of a picnic. How had her life spiraled so out of control in such a short time? Damn, she'd spent years putting scandal and bad publicity behind her. Now, she'd been dropped right in the middle of a situation she hadn't done anything to create. It was damned humbling. The sudden realization the car had stopped moving shocked her back to the moment.

"Israel is right—you are as brilliant as you are beautiful." Bronx didn't wait for her to respond before getting out of the car. When she started to open her door, he frowned at her over the hood. Offering her his hand when the door was opened, he helped her out of the low car.

"Thank you, you're a wonderful gentleman. I'm sure your mother would be very proud." His eyes glittered with emotion as he looked down at her.

"I sure hope so, but to be honest, it was our dad who taught the rules of chivalry to his sons. Most of them, by example, but a few required knocking our heads together."

Tucking her hand into the crook of his elbow, Bronx escorted her into a dress shop, Bristol hadn't even known existed. A woman in a rose-colored dress, Bristol knew cost more than her entire wardrobe, rushed to greet Bronx without even looking twice at her. When Bristol tensed, Bronx tightened his hold on her hand.

"Mr. Adler, what a wonderful surprise. I've seen you on television… your ads are always delightfully entertaining. I must say, you are even more handsome in person. I heard your brother was in town for a wedding. I'm sure you enjoyed spending time with your family. What can I show you?" The woman was fawning over him to the point, it was almost funny. Bristol was making sucking noises in her mind when she heard Israel's laughter float through her mind.

You'll get used to it, Beautiful. Women fall over Bronx and Kensington. The rest of us have just learned to use it to our advantage.

Knowing Israel had been able to stay connected to her despite the distance between them was impressive, but realizing Israel went to the trouble when she suspected he was busy, warmed her heart. Damn, he wasn't playing fair.

I don't intend to play fair, mate. I intend to win. Your heart is the prize.

By the time Bristol realized Israel had cut the connection, Bronx was standing in front of her, smiling.

"Are you ready to spend some of my brother's money, sweetness? Israel already called to let the staff here know we were coming. Seems he gave them some pretty clear guidance about what he has in mind." When she started to speak, he shook his head. "Choose your battles, Bristol. Israel wants to do this for you. Gratitude is so much nicer than protesting. Accepting a gift doesn't make you any less independent."

"But… the clothes here…" Lowering her voice until it was little more than a notch below a whisper, she explained, "Everything is going to be expensive in a store like this." She picked up a delicate camisole, folded neatly on a nearby table and gasped. "I'd be scared to wear anything costing more than my monthly rent."

"Darlin', I've seen your apartment. Whatever you were paying was too much." Bristol probably should have been insulted by the judgment, but he was right. The little studio was a dump… but until today, it had always felt relatively safe. "I'm not as gifted an empath as my brother, but I've spent my entire professional career reading people, so I've gotten pretty good at it." Pulling her into a quick hug, he kissed the top of her head and chuckled. "We're going to have a long chat about your business manager situation. I understand saving money—but damn, girl—that apartment was a fucking slum box." His disarming smile and sense of humor put her at ease.

"Can we compromise? Maybe get some things I won't be terrified to wear?" Shaking his head, he led her back to the dressing rooms.

"Here's my offer for a compromise. We buy what Israel requested—after all, these ladies work on commission. You don't want to be responsible for their heartbreak, do you?"

"I'm not sure how this is a compromise." Bristol understood she was being manipulated but knew it was useless to resist.

"While you're trying on everything in the dressing room, I'll text my staff to get the names of a few more moderately priced boutiques." She firmed her mouth into a hard line—this didn't seem like much of a compromise, but his take-or-leave-it shrug told her she'd be wasting her time to plead her case. "Perfect. I love a fast learner. Now, go on. The sooner we get this done, the sooner we can hit the steak house. I'm starving."

Five hours later, Bristol shuffled like a zombie, following Bronx into his favorite steakhouse. She had no idea how or why women enjoyed spending their entire day shopping. Her feet ached from trying on shoes until they all started to blur together. The whole process was exhausting, and she worried after the first hour, points were being shaved off her IQ. Who cared if her purse matched her shoes or her shoes were within the same color family as her outfit? Lord love a leprechaun.

At one point, she'd asked one of the sales associates if there was an app for her phone with some sort of spreadsheet to help her remember which accessories went with each outfit. She could finance a small country with the amount of money they spent today.

The bargain shops his staff suggested were marginally better, but the clothing was still far more expensive than anything she'd ever owned. When she'd argued she didn't have a large enough closet for everything they were buying, Bronx has laughed.

"Everything is being delivered to Israel's place. If you decide he's an ogre, I'm sure Austin and Asia will be happy to give you a suite of your own—but I wouldn't count on Israel going for it."

Making their way to the bar, Bristol was surprised to see Israel and Catalina seated across from each other in a high-backed leather booth. Both had their backs against the wall, so their gazes could easily sweep the large room. Israel got to his feet, holding out his hand to her. As soon as she placed her palm against his, Israel frowned at his brother.

"She's exhausted. Did you feed her anything or just run her ragged shopping?" Bristol felt the arc of electricity pass between them, Israel's much stronger than hers.

"It's not Bronx's fault. He was very patient, and I wasted a lot of his time arguing about how much money we were spending." Israel continued to glare at his brother as he helped her slide into the booth, placing himself between her and the room. A vision of her destroyed apartment flashed through her mind, the memory sending a shudder of foreboding up her spine. "Thank you for dealing with Chief Andrews. I need to contact my insurance agent, but I doubt the damage will be more than my deductible."

"That was on my list, sister. All done. They'll be sending you a check. The paperwork is in Israel's office." Bristol felt her eyes widen at Catalina's comments. How had she had time to take care of Bristol's business when she was busy getting her jewelry line and shop up and running? There was no way Bristol would ever be able to afford one of Catalina's original designs, but the pieces she'd seen online were breathtaking.

"Thank you. I appreciate you taking the time to make the calls when I know you're busy with your own business." She was shocked to her core to learn she'd be getting any money.

"No problem. When I learned who your agent was, I volunteered. He was a classmate of London's and had a huge crush on her. He was a jock, and she was a nerd. I never did understand the attraction, but it turns out, he's still a big fan of hers, so I played the family card for all it was worth. His new wife moved to Austin a month ago, and it seems the waiting list for appointments with Dr. B is long... *very long*, according to Ted. You can probably expect him to call in the favor sooner rather than later."

Bristol shrugged, trying to look unaffected by the Adlers' show of solidarity. Having them helping her felt wonderful and terrifying at the same time. Gulping several large swallows of the frozen margarita sitting in front of her, Bristol felt the rush of the alcohol before realization hit her.

"Fudge, I hope this is mine."

Chapter Ten

ISRAEL WAS GRATEFUL Bristol had the opportunity to spend several hours with Bronx. His brother was smart, intuitive, and a natural salesman. He'd talked to Bronx several times during the day and knew how reluctant she'd been to spend money. While he appreciated her conservative nature, he also wanted her to have the things she needed and deserved. Israel was still furious, someone had destroyed everything in her apartment.

There wasn't any doubt the intruder had been a shifter, but he hadn't wanted to confirm the questions he'd heard streaming through Bristol's mind. Equally clear was the shifter was someone they knew because he or she had tried to cover their scent by dumping an entire bottle of nasty smelling perfume everywhere. Fortunately, the perpetrator had used a brand containing a large percentage of alcohol. Once the alcohol fully evaporated, underlying scents were easily detected.

Although the scent was familiar, he couldn't confirm the other shifter's identity. The first person he intended to check was Clovia Williams. Parker wouldn't be able to charge her based on Israel's identification, but she would face censure within the shifter community.

Shifters as a group were supportive of each other out of necessity. Fighting among themselves led to their discovery by nonmagicals, which inevitably ended in public exposure. Historically, being revealed publicly as a shifter meant you were either forced to flee, leaving everything behind, or you risked being lynched by an angry mob of torch-bearing villagers, intent on ridding their communities of anything they didn't understand.

Recently, popular movies brought new levels of under-standing of members of their communities, but most government officials were a different story. The local police chief was more open-minded than most and discrete enough to wait until they were alone to ask the important questions.

A sharp kick to his shin brought Israel back to the mo-ment. He glared at his sister, but Cat wasn't the least bit intimidated. She returned his glower with one of her own before flashing him an unrepentant grin.

"You are not the boss of me, so you can stuff the dirty looks, little brother."

What a load of bullshit. She's only a year older and still lord-ing it over me.

"You're a menace, Catalina. Cooper is doing a lousy job of keeping you in line. Where is he anyway?" The shift in Cat's expression was so subtle, only someone who knew her well would have noticed the small tells—the inconspic-uous tensing of her jaw and the flash of concern reflected in her wary eyes. Israel felt his brows pull together when he noticed Cat rubbing the fabric napkin between her fin-gers—a nervous gesture she'd had since she was a kid. He knew she'd worked hard to break the habit—he also knew it only resurfaced when Catalina was skating on the edge of an emotional implosion.

"He was called away on business." *I can't tell you any more about this. Leave it alone, Is.* Her use of the nickname only his siblings used had the desired effect. He backed off—for now. Bronx broke the tension by wrapping an arm around Cat, giving her an affectionate squeeze.

"I'm glad Cooper's out of town. Hell, I already know there isn't a chance in the world the beautiful woman I spent the day with is going to be interested in barhopping." Looking at Catalina, he flashed a smile Israel knew made every woman on the planet melt. "You're pinch-hitting tonight, Cat."

Israel knew the two of them wouldn't be barhopping. Bronx was experiencing a security issue at one of his dealerships and was hoping Catalina could help him catch the culprit. So far, the intruder hadn't taken anything and was never seen clearly enough on any of the security cameras to make an identification. Dodging the large number of cameras Israel, which installed at all the dealerships, made them believe they were dealing with a magical. No one knew who was managing to breach every security measure they put in place or what they wanted since nothing was ever disturbed or missing.

"Well, would you look at that? Someone drank my margarita." Looking up at him, Bristol's blue eyes appeared slightly unfocused as they narrowed. "Was it you? That seems a bit presump... umm precou... shit... pushy. Yeah, that's it. Pushy. I'm still thirsty. Can I have another since I didn't get to drink this one?"

Damn, she'd only had one drink, and his mate was

trashed. If he didn't get some food in her, she was going to be down for the count. He looked up, grateful to see their waiter approaching with their dinner.

"You can have another drink after you finish your dinner." The imp had the audacity to look to Bronx for help.

"Do something. I'm thirsty, and your brother is being mean. Hell, I didn't like the parents I had... why would I want to give fate another shot at blowing up my heart."

Shit. Even drunk, she'd managed to paint him into a corner. If he hadn't been worried about her getting sick, he might have relented. Luckily, she saved him the trouble. Israel laughed when her focus switched to the steak in front of her.

"Holy cow." She burst out laughing at the unintentional pun. "Rare. Perfect. Hey, wait. Somebody put a potato on the plate with my steak. Who would do such a thing? At least they didn't try to give me a salad. That would have been insulting." Shoveling in several small pieces of steak into her mouth, Israel heard her moan. Damned if the sound didn't go straight to his cock. "I love steak. I don't get to eat it often, my budget doesn't have room for steaks, and before this past week, my schedule was a train wreck, too." Between bites, she kept chattering, making the rest of them laugh.

She's said more now than she did the entire time we were shopping. Margaritas are going to be the magic elixir to get her to open up, brother.

Even though the observation had been telepathic, Israel was still able to hear the affection and amusement in Bronx's voice. When the waiter brought Bristol another margarita, her smile lit up the room.

"Thank you, I appreciate it. I'm always in awe of food service workers. You all are amazing."

The young man paused for a heartbeat, and Israel suspected the steakhouse patrons were usually too engrossed in their business or romantic discussions to thank those serving them. Bristol's simple act of kindness told him more about her character than anything in his staff's report. Hell, maybe he needed to start taking people out for a drink before interviewing them. The young man smiled, nodding his thanks before disappearing into the kitchen once again.

"I worked at a bar the summer before I started medical school—hardest job in the world. Drug names are scientific, they make sense. Drinks? Not so much. Seriously, naming a drink Sex on the Beach doesn't tell you it has vodka, peach schnapps, grapefruit, and cranberry juice in it." When none of them responded, she simply shrugged. "You have to learn the ingredients and amounts. Hell, the only reason it isn't worse than cooking is even I couldn't find a way to set something on fire. No risk of burning the place down should have made it the perfect summer job. I guess it wasn't that bad—aside from having to pay one of my classmates to create a fake ID. I didn't drink, I was there for work. Why did I need to be twenty-one? Another ridiculous rule. Have you noticed there are a lot of insane rules these days? It's like that old song by the Five Man Electrical Band... *Sign, sign, everywhere a sign. Blockin' out the scenery, breakin' my mind. Do this, don't do that. Can't you read the sign?*"

Taking another large gulp of her drink, Bristol shrugged when no one else at the table spoke, just stared at her, their mouths hanging open in surprise.

They didn't even try to sing along, what's up with that? Oh, well, not my problem. Letting the alcohol take the edge off this dumpster-fire of a day feels better than I imagined it could. Damn, being able to speak my mind is damned liberating. Sort of like those women back in the sixties burning their bras... not like anyone would notice if I burned mine, but... Wait, where was I going with this?

Her mind had been spinning, and the only thing he'd been able to piece together had him battling laughter. It was time to reel her back in a bit.

"I noticed you didn't have much in your kitchen, Beautiful." What little she had was now in the apartment complex dumpster. He hadn't felt bad about throwing away the broken dishes since nothing seemed to be of any particular significance.

"I never really learned to cook. During college, I wasn't allowed to cook in my dorm room." Taking a big drink of her margarita, she looked at the baked potato and sighed. "I supposed I could eat another one." When Cat snickered, obviously understanding Bristol's reluctance. "I had a small microwave in my room. I wasn't allowed to make popcorn after the fire. Turns out, you actually need to pay attention to microwave popcorn, or the bag catches on fire, and the stench is nasty. Who knew? I ate so many baked potatoes, I swore I'd never be able to choke down another one."

"Oh, we're going to get along great, sister. Cooking is not in my skill set, either. Hell, now that I think about it, none of the women in my circle of friends cook. I have to give my mom credit, she had a lot more luck teaching the boys to cook than she did with her daughters." Israel heard the longing in Cat's voice. They all missed their parents as much today as they did when they first lost them. The pain wasn't as acute now, but the dull ache was always lurking just below the surface.

Israel had recently learned a couple of members of a neighboring pack were overheard discussing how they'd taken out the head of Adler Oil and his witchy wife once and would do it again—for a price. So far, the information was little more than a rumor. Two drunks bragging in a bar wasn't credible evidence, but it wasn't something he planned to ignore.

Bristol turned to him so quickly, her blonde hair fanned out around her, and in his mind's eye, he saw it spread over his bare thighs as she wrapped her lips around the head of his cock. Hell, the rush made him dizzy.

"It's cool that your mom taught you to cook." A look of panic flashed in her eyes before she started frantically digging in her small purse. "Shit. What was I thinking? I shouldn't be drinking? I better call someone about… something. What time is it? I know I have to be late for something. I'm always late."

She was spiraling, winding herself up so tight, energy was pouring from her. Putting his hand on her forearm to still her frantic digging, Israel was shocked by the fear he felt from her. She was terrified she was letting her patients down and even more worried about being impaired.

"Bristol, listen to me. We talked about this earlier. Your shift is being covered. Parker called the hospital, and they shared our concerns about your safety, especially after we discovered one of the alarms at your clinic was triggered last night." She gasped, spinning to look at Bronx, her eyes narrowing.

"No, sweetness, I didn't know anything about it until just now. I know my brother—I'll bet you dollars to doughnuts, he wanted to make sure you ate something before he shared information, he knew would upset you." She didn't respond for so long, Israel was beginning to worry she was slipping through his fingers.

"This has been the strangest day." Bristol leaned back and sighed. Her expression was more resigned than worried, and Israel could feel the sadness he'd known was coming. She drained the last of her margarita and shook her head. "I should have gotten the security system with cameras, but I didn't have the money at the time. We haven't had any trouble, so I've never upgraded it. I'll call someone tomorrow."

Catalina and Bronx both burst out laughing, no doubt their amusement being fed by the stricken look on Israel's face.

"Damn, I'd have paid good money to have that on video. You've just achieved hero status with the Adler sisters, Bristol. Now, in the interest of saving your ass some serious time over Israel's lap, you might want to speak with him about your security needs rather than calling another firm."

Catalina's coaching gave Israel time to pull back his frustration. The truth was, they'd only met a couple of days earlier, so it wasn't a huge surprise she'd forgotten what he did for a living. Not to mention she'd had a damned stressful day, topped off with an impressive amount of alcohol.

"I didn't forget you have a security company, but it

would be presumptuous—see, I do know how to say that word—for me to assume you want to provide services." She must have sensed the sudden chill in the air because her expression became wary as she cut herself off. "Not those services, good heavens, I'd never..." Her face went scarlet, and her eyes dilated as the magnitude of her error worked its way to the surface of her alcohol-infused mind. Bristol's thoughts were spinning so frantically, she hadn't noticed the couple who'd walked in and were standing beside their table.

"Oh, dear. I recognize that look. A sub who's had too much alcohol and just stepped off a bridge into shit up to their eyeballs." As usual, Asia Adler had summed things up perfectly. Her knack for cutting to the bottom line was just one of the reasons her reputation as Adler Oil's legal eagle was well earned. Bristol's gaze jerked to Franklin Cordesi, before turning to Asia. "Girl, you are too impaired to be pulling a tiger's tail. Let me give you a bit of free legal advice. *Stop talking.* Don't apologize because he isn't going to buy it."

Bristol stared up at Asia, who was standing beside their table. Blinking slowly once, then again, trying to bring the second oldest Adler into focus, Bristol wondered how long they'd been standing there.

Asia switched her attention to Israel, her eyes narrowing enough to let him know she wasn't pleased. The two of them had always been close. Asia was one of the few people whose opinion of him mattered—usually, he let criticism roll off like water on a duck's back.

Rein in your temper, Israel. She's new. It doesn't matter she's been a member of the club for a while—she hasn't played enough to understand one of the nuances of submitting to your Dom is asking for his help.

"*Cara*, you know the rules." Franklin didn't like his wife communicating telepathically in private—it didn't matter she was reading Israel the riot act. Cordesi had lived all over the world, but hints of his upper-crust upbringing only made their way to the surface when he was dealing with Asia. Israel joked, coping with her required so much focus, Franklin wasn't able to monitor his tells. His brother-in-law had simply nodded his agreement.

Bristol picked up her empty margarita glass and licked the rim to get the last drop, making everyone laugh. Israel wasn't sure if she'd been trying to break the tension or get the waiter's attention. He shook his head and set the glass back on the table.

"No more for you, Beautiful. I suspect you aren't going to feel so frisky in the morning. It's time to get you home." He tossed more than enough cash on the table to cover the tab and a generous tip before pulling Bristol to her feet. She swayed, making her mutter a few words he planned to eliminate from her vocabulary. Turning to his family, he cautioned Bronx and Cat to be careful with their investigation.

"Thanks for babysitting me today, Bronx. You're a sweetheart."

Israel reminded himself it was his own fault his mate spent the day bonding with his brother. Their friendship was harmless, and the bond was beneficial for several reasons, but her words still sent jealousy rocketing through him.

"Holy hand-painted horny toads, did you just growl at

me? It's not nice to growl at people, Israel. It makes them think they've done something wrong when they haven't." She hiccupped and had the good sense to appear at least marginally contrite. "I learned that in Psychology 101, and there was a refresher chapter in Social Psychology. Let me guess, you skipped as many humanities classes as possible."

"Oh, hell, I like her. I like her a lot." Catalina took a sip of her wine, then lifted the glass into the air, toasting the curvy beauty leaning against him.

Cat had seemed distracted when he picked her up, and Israel caught her checking her phone several times during dinner. She hadn't spoken to anyone or replied to any messages, so he assumed whoever she was waiting to hear from hadn't contacted her. Israel presumed Cooper Hicks was the culprit, but he wasn't going to get involved unless she asked for his help.

"Doms are always preaching, *begin as you intend to go*, and I say subs need to do the same. If you start tolerating growly behavior, you'll be stuck putting up with that crap forever. Don't let him start disappearing in the middle of the night, either."

Israel was surprised by Cat's comment. He'd never heard her make any observation—positive or negative—about the lifestyle, but it was her remark about disappearing in the middle of the night he found disturbing. Damn it all to hell, just when he'd vowed to not get involved.

I'll talk to her. Take your mate home, she needs some serious pampering and rest.

Israel knew Bronx was right. Pampering and rest were on the agenda—right after he introduced her to the joys of erotic spanking. Bristol might appear relaxed, courtesy of

Jose Cuervo, but he could feel the spring inside her winding tighter and tighter. He planned to give her a more satisfying way to relieve the stress, he knew would make them both happy.

Chapter Eleven

B RISTOL TOOK ISRAEL'S outstretched hand, letting him help her from the car. The drive from the steak house to Adler Oil wasn't long, but the cooler night air sobered her enough, she knew better than to insist on doing everything herself. He no longer appeared angry, but his rigid posture and the tight set of his jaw told her Israel wasn't in the mood for arguments. He led her into the elevator, tapped in the code giving him access to the private floor where his suite was located, then pinned her against the mirrored wall.

Shackling her wrists above her head with one hand, he used the index finger of his free hand to draw a line along the underside of her jaw. Goosebumps raced up her arms as she felt her nipples draw into tight peaks. Moisture warmed her sex, and someone moaned—it might have been her. He pressed his knee between her thighs, putting enough pressure on her clit to tease, but not enough to push her over.

"You're so responsive. Seeing the way your body reacts to my touch is so fucking hot." The elevator door slid open, but he didn't seem to be in a hurry to exit. Pressing a button on the control panel, he locked the door open and grinned. "We have two minutes before the alarm sounds. Let's not waste it." His lips sealed over hers, firm and demanding with a note of tenderness that touched her soul. Desire moved through her in a rolling wave more devastating than she could have imagined. When she tried to tilt her hips forward, the damned man chuckled.

"As much as I want you, I'm not fucking you until we've had a chat about expectations. Don't get me wrong, I'm looking forward to taking you to the club and showing you off—all in good time, Beautiful."

Expectations? Good grief. She would be happy to tell him what she'd expected—relief from the fire he'd stoked. Damn, what was the point of getting her all excited, then shutting her down?

The only reason any man will ever want you is for your brain because nobody is going to give two shits about your fat ass, girl.

Bristol heard her mother's words play in her mind, just as they had any time one of the Doms at the club asked her to play. Taking a deep breath, Bristol nodded, stepping behind the emotional wall she'd learned to erect as a child. The barrier was bulletproof and always protected her from the emotional badgering she'd endured until she'd become so focused on building her medical practice, there hadn't been any time for other people's nonsense.

Bristol heard a disembodied voice warning them the elevator would notify the local authorities in thirty seconds, but she was too busy reminding herself, she shouldn't be surprised to care. The walk down the hall to his suite felt more like a trip to the gallows, and she found herself slowing until Israel finally wrapped his hand around hers to pull her along.

"As soon as the door closes behind us, I want you na-ked."

Seriously? What the hell? Shutting me out a couple of minutes ago wasn't enough, he's going for round two?

ISRAEL WANTED TO track down the asshole who'd destroyed his mate's confidence. He knew she had faith in her professional abilities, but she was fucking clueless about how much he wanted her. Banking his frustration, Israel was determined to give his mate what she needed rather than what she'd wanted in the elevator. If he'd taken her there, she'd have dismissed it as nothing more than lust, and in the process, written him off as a mate.

"Bristol, the door is closed, why aren't you naked?" Her startled expression told him she hadn't believed he was serious. She'd soon learn he always meant what he said during a scene. When they were simply enjoying each other's company in a casual setting, Israel could tease with the best of them. As a Dom, he kept his comments as open and honest as possible. Safe, Sane, and Consensual might be the guiding tenet of the BDSM lifestyle, but trust was the foundation solid D/s relationships were built on.

"Could we turn the lights down?" *Or Off? Off would be better.*

Israel wasn't sure he'd ever seen a submissive strip slower than Bristol was moving. It had taken her a full thirty seconds to toe-off her shoes, for Goddess' sake.

"No, Beautiful. I want to be able to see every inch of your lovely body. As your mate and Dom, it's my right and privilege to look at what belongs to me." He took a step back, spread his feet shoulder-width apart, crossing his arms over his well-muscled chest. The pose was unmistakably dominant, the shift in body language, sending a message no trained submissive would miss.

"Geez, Louise, I should have had another margarita."

Israel bit the inside of his cheeks to keep from laughing out loud at Bristol's muttered words. She might think the extra drink would have given her more courage, but he knew better. Another drink and he'd have had to carry her out of the steakhouse, and they wouldn't be playing. Bristol's mind was questioning the sincerity of his attraction, but thankfully, her body was miles ahead of the game.

"Stop thinking and move, Beautiful. My plans for tonight do not include punishment, so get your lovely ass in gear." Israel looked forward to seeing her bare derriere lying over his lap, cheeks blushing under his hand. He hoped Bristol would be brave enough to skate along the fine line between pleasure and pain. Not all submissives understood the sensations were two sides of the same coin, but for those who *got it*, their sexual pleasure was magnified exponentially. In the future, he wouldn't allow her to dawdle, but tonight, he was having fun watching her pull strength from within to face her insecurities.

Blowing out a breath when she was finally undressed, Bristol kept her eyes on her pink-tipped toes. Refusing to look him in the eye was just another way to hide, and he wasn't going to allow it. Bristol needed to see the appreciation he knew was shining in his eyes. Damn, the woman was a fucking goddess, and she had no clue.

"Eyes on me, Beautiful." Bristol lifted her face so slowly, he swore he needed photos to be sure she was moving. Nodding his approval when she finally met his gaze, he was grateful he'd forced the issue. Her quick inhalation was all the reassurance he needed—his mate had seen herself through his eyes for the first time. When she blushed, he shook his head.

"I love the way your expression tells me what you're thinking. As tantalizing as I find the pink flush on your cheeks, I won't tolerate you being embarrassed about your body. I want you to see yourself as I see you."

Their telepathic connection was growing stronger by the hour. The deeper he could forge the bond between them, the sooner he'd be able to claim her. Israel could hardly wait for the moment she tilted her head to the side, signally she was ready to be his. The two puncture wounds from his bite would heal under the lap of his tongue, sealing closed immediately, leaving behind small round scars most people would never notice, and even fewer would correctly identify.

The exchange of their DNA would bring significant enhancement to both of their magical skills. He'd be able to track her anywhere in the world and would instinctively know if she was in danger. Mating affected shifter pairs in different ways, some more significantly than others. He couldn't wait to find out what changes were in store for them.

"Turn around, face the window, spread your feet as far apart as you can comfortably, and lace your fingers together at the back of your head." She moved into position quickly, but the alcohol made it difficult to move her feet as far apart as he suspected she would be able to manage without Jose's help.

"Gorgeous." Using his finger, he traced an invisible line from her shoulder down, curving around to her upper ribs, continuing slowly to her waist. Israel opened his hand, pressing his warm palm over Bristol's silky skin, letting the pads of his fingers press firmly against her as he fanned her lush curves.

"I love your curves. You are real and perfect. The thought of holding a stick in my arms holds no appeal. Most of the men I know prefer women who are rounded and pillowy soft as we push ourselves in as deep as our cocks can go. Feeling your breasts flatten against my chest when my cock is buried to the hilt will be one of my greatest joys. Knowing those breasts will one day feed our children adds more to the attraction than you know. I guarantee, my brother watches Charlotte nurse their child every chance he gets. It's an intimate pleasure he won't want to share with anyone else, not because he is ashamed or embarrassed, but because it's his alone."

Moving his hand to cup the underside of her breast, Israel brushed his thumb over the tip of her nipple.

"Look at how your body responds to my touch. There is nothing better. Bristol, you have no idea how perfect you are for me. Fate doesn't make mistakes. I know the timing doesn't always make sense to us—it isn't always convenient—but it's always *right*."

Bristol's thoughts had been spinning so fast, Israel had barely been able to catch a word here and there. Her mind was bouncing ideas around like a steel ball in the old-fashioned pinball machines he'd enjoyed so much as a kid—every thought remaining unfocused until he mentioned timing. One word brought it all to a halt. Bristol zeroed in on his comment, trying to find a way around his observation without success. He could tell she wasn't convinced but couldn't come up with a valid argument.

"Why me? You could have any woman you wanted." Technically, her comment wasn't that far off the mark. He'd had plenty of women over the years. Israel could walk into any bar in the city and leave with the woman of his choice. He shook his head and smiled.

"You may be a shifter, but you seem to be awfully na-ïve about the way things work. You and Denali are cut from the same cloth, baby. She's been thrown into the deep end of learning, too. It'll be a remarkably interesting conversation, but we're saving it for another day." He didn't plan to waste this time with her, chit-chatting about his newest sister-in-law.

"Come." Taking her hand, Israel led Bristol around the end of one of the designer sofas in the living room. *Who on earth thought that thing would be relaxing to sit on?* He'd enjoyed sitting on park benches more than the uncomfortable, overpriced piece of designer furniture. Picking up the chair he planned to use, Israel deliberately set it, so his right side was toward the large sliding glass doors leading to the deck.

"What is your safe word, Bristol?" To her credit, she didn't pretend the question had been unclear.

"Red, Sir." She'd answered with enough bravado to make him wonder if it was sincere or alcohol-fueled. *I guess we'll see soon enough.*

"I don't believe you'll need it, but it's an important reminder for both of us. People sometimes have triggers they aren't aware of, things that send them reeling physically or emotionally. If you find yourself approaching one of those points, say *yellow*. I'll stop, and we'll talk about what's happening, giving you an opportunity to tell me what part of our scene you're struggling with. I may completely stop, or change things up, or in some cases I will simply continue on. But, I promise to listen to your concerns with an open mind. If the situation is too much for you and you know it will be impossible for you to go forward, say *red*. Your safe word will always work." *Always*.

"Tell me you understand, Beautiful."

"I understand, Sir. Yellow for slow down and red for stop."

Israel loved the airy tone her voice had taken on. Getting her in the right headspace was critical to the success of the scene he planned. Brilliant women were both a joy and a challenge to their Doms. Helping them escape their racing minds, even if the reprieve was brief, was described by subs as the greatest gift they ever received. Dominants lucky enough to top those women cherished the gift of their sub's trust. Making your way into those gifted minds wasn't easy, but the rewards were enormous.

"I want to try an experiment, Beautiful. Let's see how your body responds to erotic spanking." Without giving her time to protest, Israel pulled her over his lap, peaking her bare ass in position for his palm to land in heated strokes. She sucked in a breath, preparing to protest when he cut it off with two solid swats, designed to get her attention but not hurt. "Before you complain, stop and think about what you're feeling. Don't listen to your head—tune out the voice telling you what you should be feeling and listen closely to what your body is saying."

Two more swats on each cheek were all he managed

before the musky scent of her arousal filled the air. *Perfect.* Upping the intensity each time his palm landed on her beautiful ass, he felt her relax a little more. This woman was made for him. Slipping his fingers between her thighs, Israel was thrilled to find her soaked.

"It's going to be damned hard to convince me you aren't enjoying this, Bristol. You're fucking drenched, and I couldn't be happier." Pushing two fingers into her vagina, Israel smiled to himself when her muscles tightened around him, pulling him deeper, trying to keep him from moving away.

"Please." The whispered plea was so faint, even with his enhanced hearing, Israel barely heard it. It was unlikely she'd meant to speak aloud, even less, she fully understood what she was asking for.

"Tell me what you need, Beautiful." He knew—hell, it was pulsing off her in delicious waves—but it was important for her to put her feelings into words. Verbalizing what her body craved would go a long way to her understanding how fulfilling submission could be. Israel loved watching the look of astonishment on a new submissive's face when they discovered the pure pleasure they could find when they let their bodies lead. Social conventions were so narrow, those new to the lifestyle rarely understood how sweet pain could be.

"More. I don't know why. I'm not able to think enough to figure it out, but I know there has to be more."

There is so much more, baby. Let's up everything a notch, shall we?

Opening the top drawer on a nearby end table, Israel pulled out a couple of toys he'd hidden inside before heading out to the steak house. Using his legs, Israel lifted her ass until her legs slid apart several inches, giving him the extra space he needed. Pulling his fingers from her slick vagina, he used her juices to tease her rear entrance. She clenched her ass cheeks, giving him the perfect excuse to land a couple of stinging swats on her already cherry red flesh.

"Don't even think about it. Relax those muscles and let me play with your pretty ass." When she drew in a deep breath, Israel took advantage of her moment of distraction to push a finger past the tight ring of outer muscles. "There are so many nerve endings here—the potential for pleasure is off-the-chart." Using his finger to slowly fuck her rear hole, he felt her juices soak through the lightweight fabric of his dress slacks. His cock was so hard, he wondered if it would burst through his zipper in a quest for relief.

"It feels... so naughty. I'm not supposed to like this."

"Why? Because some uptight schoolmarm told you anal pleasure would send you into the fiery depths of hell?" He'd heard the same refrain so many times. Who the hell was talking to young people about sex, anyway? He kept imagining the nuns from the old Haley Mills movies his sisters used to watch on TBS. Hell, those movies had to be from the 1960s, but the girls loved the antics of Mills' character at the convent school.

"Nobody talked to me about sex, except to say *don't do it* until I was in medical school." Holy hell, Israel wanted to slap his palm against his forehead. He'd read her file and should have known better. "It's okay. I didn't... well, I didn't have a normal childhood." She was speaking casually, as though he wasn't working to relax the vice-like grip her anal passage had on his finger as he used it to fuck her ass. Before she'd finished speaking, Bristol was lifting her sweet backside into his touch. Pulling his hand from her body, Israel felt the loss immediately.

Coating a small plug with lube, Israel inserted the tip and kept up a steady pressure, unrelenting in his intent to seat it in his mate's sweet ass. The plug was the smallest one he'd been able to find in his favorite shop. The small device would do little to prepare her for anal sex, other than introduce her to the sensual pleasure of having something in her ass. When he was balls deep in her, Israel would use the tiny remote to turn on the slender plug, and the vibrations would amplify the experience for both of them.

"Push all those stereotypes out of your mind, Beautiful. Let your body guide you. There is no room for embarrassment or shame between us."

She nodded stiffly.

She hadn't used words, something he wouldn't always allow, but tonight was going to be an exception to many of the usual rules of protocol. His mate's lack of experience in submission was eclipsed only by her sexual inexperience. Israel understood the importance of balancing her introduction to the lifestyle with the tamer elements of sex most people are exposed to in college and early adulthood.

It was ironic, as a gynecologist and obstetrician, Bristol advised patients on sexual topics she'd never personally experienced. Israel wondered if her input would change as she gained *hands-on experience*. Giving her ass a heated pat, Israel kept his hand in place, letting the heat from his palm intensify the sting.

"It's different with the plug." He loved hearing the airy quality of her voice. His mate's arousal was a powerful aphrodisiac. There was a sing-song quality to her voice when she was sexually aroused, nothing like the fact-based physician, dealing with Charlotte at the club.

"Good different or bad different?"

"Oh, so good. It's absolutely delicious. The swat pushed it just deep enough to remind me it's there. I've heard the other subs talk about plugs, but I had the impression they were much larger."

Israel couldn't hold back his laughter. He could only imagine what the other submissives at the club had told her. It was terrifying to think about Bristol in the women's locker room with Tobi West or Jen McCall. Hell, what was he thinking? His sisters would be able to coach her on all the ways to annoy him. Maybe he needed to rethink his plan to take Bristol to the club tomorrow night.

"If it's all the same to you—I'd like to finish what you started before thinking about the club. I really need to come. My entire body is on fire." She was grinding herself against him, pressing against his aching cock, and making it damned hard for him to think of anything but the overwhelming desire to fuck her.

"You'll get five swats for trying to top from the bottom. We move on my timetable, not yours, Beautiful." Even though she'd attempted to phrase the request as respectfully as possible, it didn't matter, and it wasn't a habit he wanted to encourage. Hell, the time would give him a couple of minutes to find his damned control.

Chapter Twelve

HOLY BURNING ASS cheeks from hell. The five swats Israel gave her because she'd politely asked him to get the hell on with it, fucking hurt. They still hadn't turned to pleasure yet, and Bristol wasn't sure how she felt about that. Maybe she wasn't meant to be a sub after all. Spending the rest of her life having boring sex hurt a lot more than Israel's monster paws landing on her backside, but holy fiery hell. Damn, she hated waffling between answers.

Indecision is a decision, Bristol. She could still hear Ms. Ames's reminder. Her high school science teacher stepped up when Bristol's parents died. Althea Ames took in a high school sophomore, agreeing to look after the brilliant but angry girl, who turned ten the day her parents were buried. Ms. Ames changed Bristol's life in so many ways, she shuddered to think where she might have ended up without her. None of them had known at the time how short their time together would be. Althea knew she had cancer but hadn't told anyone, worried the judge would place Bristol in a home where she wouldn't thrive. Shaking her head, Bristol tried to push the sadness aside. It spoke volumes that she'd grieved Althea for years but hadn't felt anything but relief when her parents died.

"Let's see if I can't help you refocus on the moment, Beautiful."

Israel was above her, his cockhead pressing against her opening. Holy Hannah, she'd been so lost in the sadness of her past, she didn't remember him laying her on the bed. Israel's smile was part devilment and part promise.

"You're right about the promise. You'll soon learn I'll never make a promise I don't intend to keep. As for the devilment—well, you're right about that as well."

Holding up a small black box, Israel wiggled his eyebrows and smiled. Bristol saw him slide a switch along the top of the box a split second before he pushed his enormous cock so deep, she felt the tip press against the opening of her womb. It took her mind a couple of seconds to realize the reason it felt like her vagina was electrified.

"Fucking hell, baby. You were tight before—now it's borderline excruciating."

Bristol could hear the strain in Israel's voice. She'd seen some of the plugs the Doms at the club used—they were huge. She was starting to understand why her friends insisted fucking with a plug was a whole new experience.

"You need to catch up, Beautiful, I'm not going to last long, and I want you with me when I come."

She had big news for him—she was already spiraling over the edge so fast, he was the one lagging behind.

"Now, Bristol. Come with me."

Israel's command set off an explosive reaction beginning at her core before lighting every nerve ending on fire. Bristol's skin was tingling, and her toes curled against the Egyptian cotton sheets as pleasure, unlike anything she'd imagined possible, washed over her. The power of her orgasm was so intense, she lost herself in the brilliant white fireworks exploding behind her eyelids. Israel's lips sealed over hers before she could shout into the night. Growling deep in his chest, the vibration set off another soul-shattering release.

For a few seconds, the constant internal chatter in Bristol's mind was turned off. The silence brought with it a profound sense of peace that recharged her soul. The escape so perfect, she had no idea how she could survive without it. *Drat.* Damned if the man wasn't circumventing all her defenses.

He wasn't playing fair. He had to know how much she wanted him. It wasn't just the sex—it was also the connection, the feeling of belonging she'd longed for her entire life. As a child, she'd described it to a professor as standing on the sidewalk, watching through a window as a family enjoyed a holiday meal—everyone laughing and talking, the sound of their voices muffled by the glass and distance. Knowing she'd only be able to watch from a distance was sadder than not knowing such moments existed.

Taking a deep breath, Bristol tried to slow her racing heart by focusing on what she needed to get done. With the next several days off, she might be able to find another small apartment in a safer area while she waited for the architect to finish up the plans for her lake house. He'd been putting her off forever, and it was time for her to put some pressure on him.

Damn it all to blue bidets. I don't know why he had to keep pushing. It wasn't fair for him to try to bargain with her—he'd finish the plans if she'd have sex with him.

ISRAEL WAS CERTAIN his blood pressure had to be so far off-the-chart, his eyeballs threatened to explode. He was going to delay a conversation about the architect because he was too fucking pissed to discuss it rationally at this point. First, he needed to remind her there was no reason to look for an apartment—hell, he thought the issue had already been resolved. Apparently, she hadn't thought he was serious when he said she could stay with him.

"I'm looking forward to having you here with me, Beautiful. This apartment is large enough for the two of us, so there is no need for you to worry about finding a place." He felt her stiffen against him and smiled down at her before rolling to the side, keeping them face to face.

"I'll pay rent." *As long as it isn't too much.* Who was she kidding? An apartment like this was way out of her price range.

"Are you trying to earn another punishment?" When her eyes widened, he reminded himself how new she was to the lifestyle. "You will not pay rent to me or anyone else associated with Adler Oil. That is not up for discussion. We are destined mates, Bristol. I realize the timing isn't right for you, but fate never makes a mistake. If you will stop and think about it, you'll probably be able to think of a couple of reasons we might have met now rather than later."

Israel could feel Bristol trying to step back emotionally. There were times he would allow her time to regroup, but it certainly wasn't happening when they were discussing their future. Hell, he was still deep inside her—not a good time for a submissive to try to step back from his or her Dom.

"I don't mean to seem ungrateful for all your help or disrespectful about mating. I just thought I would have more time to explore myself and the world around me without the responsibilities that accompany a full-time relationship."

Israel waited, making an effort to stay patient while she sorted through her thoughts. He could feel her struggling to put her feelings into words. He already knew she was losing the battle to resist mating. After all, he'd meant what he said... *fate never makes a mistake.*

"For so many years, I was controlled by parents who had no idea what to do with me. I'm not being boastful, but I passed them intellectually by the time I started school. It was easier for them to ignore me than figure out what I needed. Once I was in school, the powers that be quickly discovered I was smarter than the average kid and how little my parents cared. Basically, I slept at home—that was it. The rest of the time, I was at school or spending extra time with academic coaches and tutors."

"What did you do on the weekends? Where did you spend holidays?" He'd looked forward to each school break but doubted it was true of Bristol's childhood. The Adlers might have lost their parents far too early, but they'd had amazing childhoods.

"Weekends were torture... holidays as well. Several teachers worked to send me to summer enrichment camps. I didn't fully appreciate their efforts until I was in college." She chewed on her lips and shrugged. "That's why I sponsor kids who want to go to camp. If their parents can't or won't send them, I pay for it."

Israel was thrilled to learn his amazing mate was a philanthropist. Giving back was something he and his siblings were devoted to.

"You need to work with Asia on this. Adler Oil funds several scholarship programs. I know Asia has been looking for ways to expand the effort. The two of you could do amazing things for kids." Stroking the side of her face, he watched her eyes dilate and heard the slight hitch in her breathing.

"Sweet mate, belonging to me won't stop you from exploring. You'll be gaining a travel companion who is looking forward to seeing the world through your eyes. I'll never try to hold you back, personally or professionally. I want to add to your life, not restrict it." He was speaking from his heart and hoped she understood he was sincere— if not, he planned to step the process up tomorrow night at the club.

While she used the master bath, Israel used the guest bath down the hall and still beat her back to bed.

"You cannot hide in there all night, Beautiful. I can hear your brilliant mind spinning out of control from out here." Bristol opened the door, her cheeks scarlet red with embarrassment.

"I was trying to figure out what to say. You've been so patient, nothing like Charlotte portrayed you." Her comments got Israel's attention. What the hell had his sister-in-law said about him to make his mate so wary. She obviously sensed his concern because she immediately started shaking her head, "No, it wasn't what you're thinking." She walked over to the bed, sitting where he'd pulled the coverlet back for her. "She told me you and Austin were the most determined businessmen she'd ever met. There was more to the conversation, but I'm not sure I should repeat it since it took place at my office."

"Let me guess, she described my brother as a steamroller and didn't feel I was much better." Bristol's mouth dropped open, the plump lips of her bow-shaped mouth, forming a perfect O. Damn, he was looking forward to seeing his cock slide between those rose-colored lips.

It was true, he and Austin were bulldozers when it came to business. Asia was a wrecking ball, and the youngest of them, Paris, would take you apart and put you back together in a way she found easier to manipulate. Kensington had been relentless in his acting career, holding out for the best roles and negotiating contracts his fellow actors envied—all while marching to his own drummer.

"Bristol, as a group, all the Adlers are steamrollers in our professional lives because we are driven to be successful. Remember, fate has chosen mates for us who are our perfect matches. Paris needed a mate with a personality similar to hers but stronger. Without Trinity providing balance, she is the very definition of *rushing in where angels fear to tread*. Asia needed a mate who was both intelligent, politically connected, and possessing a high level of magical ability.

"What I'm trying to tell you, in a very obscure way, is fate matches the Adlers with strong mates—mates who can go toe-to-toe with us. Mates who bring much-needed counterbalance and intellectual stimulation. Mates who challenge us in all the right ways." Pushing several strands of her white-blonde hair behind her ear, Israel relished the silky feel of the locks between his fingers and let the gesture lure her in. It was the perfect segue, allowing him to change the subject without being rude.

"I love your hair. I'll always braid it before we play in our playroom or at the club." Her eyes sparkled with interest, but he shook his head. "Not tonight. You've had a few crazy days, and I'm looking forward to holding you while you sleep." He looked pointedly at the shirt she'd found while he'd been down the hall. "Lose the shirt, mate. We sleep naked. Being skin to skin makes it easier for our bodies to synchronize. You may be a shifter, but you have a lot to learn about your own body, Beautiful."

"I've heard about the synching, but I've never experienced it. I've talked to patients who describe it as a powerful connection, a level of inner-peace they'd never experienced before."

"Take off the shirt, sweetheart, and let's find out for ourselves." He made quick work of the buttons, letting her see the appreciation in his eyes as his gaze moved over the bare skin he exposed. Watching the white cotton slide sensuously off her shoulders was so fucking hot, Israel felt his cock stiffen in response. "You keep teasing me, and it'll be a good long while before you get any rest, Bristol." When he reached for the light, she went completely still.

"I won't be able to sleep if it's completely dark in the room. It's disorienting and terrifying."

He could tell there was more to the story and suspected there was more to her parents' abuse than simple neglect. Moving from the bed, Israel turned on the soft lighting in the shower before pulling the en suite's door partially closed. Bristol's whispered thanks made his heart clench. He doubted she would ever be completely free of the lingering effects of childhood abuse but hoped he and his family could help alleviate some of the more severe impediments to her happiness.

"Being able to get my bearings without waiting for my eyes to adjust will help me go back to sleep when I wake up during the night."

Last night, Israel had assumed she woke every half-hour or so because she was in a different place. If she regularly struggled with sleep disruption, her success was even more remarkable. Climbing back into bed, Israel pulled her back against his chest, sighing in contentment when she relaxed into his embrace. His cock snuggled between the cheeks of her ass, happy to be close to heaven but resigned to letting her tender tissues recover from his intense fucking.

"Go to sleep, sweetheart. I've got you. Contrary to the way it feels, my cock isn't calling the shots. My brain is still in charge, and I know your body and mind both need rest." Israel smiled to himself. This was going to be one of his favorite parts of every day—holding his naked mate in his arms, feeling her relax as her thoughts slowed enough for him to finally track them.

So comfortable. Tired. I want to let him help, but I'm afraid. What if it's a slippery slope? It would be so easy... too easy. I'll talk to Tobi or Charlotte or Lilly.

Goddess help him if she consulted with Lilly. Smiling to himself, Israel couldn't help but wonder about the relationship between the two women. Lilly was only at the club for special events. She'd told him once, she had no desire to see her sons naked ever again.

"Their childhood was enough. My husbands don't want to see the woman they consider their daughter in her birthday suit, either."

When Israel told her, he understood her position but thought it was a shame the three of them didn't feel as though they couldn't play at the club, they'd watched their sons build, Lilly had laughed out loud.

"Oh, honey, we still play at the club—we're just choosy about when we show up. Timing is everything. So many people our age are annoyed by insomnia. Hell, my husbands and I think it's the best-damned thing ever. We have keys to Prairie Winds, and since our boys no longer live upstairs, we can come and go as we please. I swear if the apartment upstairs wasn't being utilized so often, I'd suggest the three of us move in and sell our place to a young family."

Israel had expressed interest, but now that he knew Bristol had plans to build a house on a parcel of land she'd purchased nearby, there was no way he'd ask her to change her plans. Making a mental note to talk to Kent and Kyle, Israel wondered if the sprawling home would interest Catalina and Cooper.

Yes, it would. Hold that thought, and don't mention it to Cat. I'm in a bit of a pickle right now. It's only a matter of time before all the feelers Cat's putting out give her the information she's after. When that happens, promise me you'll keep her close. I don't want her walking into the trap I know is being laid for her.

Israel was shocked. It was the first time he'd been able to hear Cooper Hicks so clearly. Trying to see through the other man's eyes, Israel heard Cooper's strained laughter.

Leave it. I called Cam, and he's sending help. Watch Catalina. She's damned good... too good, and she's getting way too close.

Israel felt the connection between them sever and wondered what kind of trouble Hicks had gotten himself into this time. Turning down the Agency's offer of employment when he'd been in college had been the smartest thing Israel had ever done. He'd seen the way Catalina changed when she'd started training and known it wasn't for him. As impressed as he was with his connection to Cooper, the significance wasn't lost on him, and it was a huge concern.

Setting all the concerns aside, Israel let his mind float and let his heartbeat and breathing synch with hers. He knew the moment she slipped into a deep sleep and sent up a silent prayer, she'd stay in the more restful level longer in his arms. She needed the rest, and he wanted her well-rested—she was going to need all the energy she could muster tomorrow. He had a full day planned for his mate.

Chapter Thirteen

C ATALINA LEANED BACK in the poolside lounger and sipped the wine cooler she'd found in Asia and Austin's tiki bar. When her sister and brother decided to add the two-story outdoor living space, none of them had foreseen how amazing the unused space would be. Asia's decision to call a pool designer and builder from Florida was the beginning of a truly off-the-wall and explosively creative team.

Austin finally stepped away from the project after Asia, the designer, and the contractor called him for a creative collaboration in the Adler Oil conference room. Having inherited the business long before he'd expected to, Austin had rebuilt the failing enterprise, turning it into the conglomerate it was today. He'd rolled his eyes and left after a half-hour discussion about tinted versus printed tile for the pool perimeter.

The process might have been brutal, but the results were stunning. Letting her gaze move over the generous space, Cat marveled at the way it completely transformed at night. The rock waterfall looked genuine, the composite material a perfect imitation in appearance at a fraction of the weight. There were even palm trees in enormous pots that could be easily rolled into protected areas during the few cold nights Austin experienced every winter. Underwater lights highlighted ripples in the water from a sudden gust of wind, and fairy lights twinkled along the walls and strung along the wall behind an intricately landscaped wall totally unlike anything Catalina had ever seen.

She'd traveled all over the world and would have assured you she couldn't be impressed. Maybe it was because it belonged to the family, or perhaps because this building always represented *home*, but her breath always caught when she stepped out of the elevator into Asia's oasis atop Adler Oil.

Her vantage point above the city streetlights gave Catalina the opportunity to enjoy the vast Texas sky. As a child, Catalina imagined the Goddess scattering sparkling diamonds on a sea of deep blue velvet. She'd scamper out her bedroom window, climb the trellis onto the room roof, and lie back, watching the sky shift as the hours passed. Imagining elaborate strings of twinkling jewels, she'd seen beautiful necklaces and bracelets where others saw worlds far removed from their own. Cat often wondered if her passion for jewelry design was rooted in those memories.

A familiar voice filled her mind. Israel's voice surprised her. She'd assume he would be busy with Bristol. Cat was thrilled her brother had found his mate and hoped the brilliant beauty wouldn't make him wait too long before agreeing to be officially claimed. In the past, she'd only been able to hear Israel when he opened the channel between them, or they were both shifted into their wolf. Sensing he hadn't intentionally opened the line of telepathic communication between them, Cat was hesitant to keep the path open. When a second voice faded in, she zeroed in on what he was saying.

Sitting up straight, Catalina strained to hear every word, hoping to find out where her lover was working. What suicide mission had the Agency sent Cooper on this time? Cat was attuned to every nuance of her lover's voice, making a mental note of the background noise, memorizing everything, so she'd be able to analyze it later. She smiled to herself when she heard Cooper complain about the feelers she'd put out and his concern she would try to get to him.

So, what's good for the goose isn't good for the gander? You can run headlong into the bowels of hell to rescue me, but don't believe I should do the same? You'll have to put those patriarchal views to rest if you plan to be my mate, Ace.

BRISTOL STARED AT what was little more than a scrap of material, draped precariously on the padded hanger Israel held. Her thoughts were triangulating between shock, disbelief, and horror. His deep chuckle had her focus shifting between the dress and the man who'd just told her this minuscule excuse for clothing was what he expected her to wear to dinner before they went to the club.

"Triangulating? Damn, I love the way your brilliant mind works. Extra point for creative vocabulary, but I'm not going to change my mind about the dress."

"Dress? That's a very liberal application of the term, don't you think?" He had to agree the garment was unlike any of the modest items he'd seen in her apartment. "I'll be arrested if I wear this out in public. You said we were going to dinner, right? I'm not a snob or anything, but I have worked hard to achieve a certain level of respect in the community, and this would jeopardize that in a big way. Huge. Ginormous."

"As your Dom and mate, what is my first concern?" Rather than pushing her, Israel wanted Bristol to sort through it on her own. He would lead the conversation, but she was too intelligent to be lectured.

"My safety?" It was humbling to think about how intelligent she was, how long she'd been a member of the Prairie Winds Club, and how much she still had to learn.

"And my second priority?" He loved seeing realization dawn in her pretty blue eyes. Damn, the woman was a treasure.

They'd spent the first half of the afternoon in the playroom before swimming and enjoying a short nap under the fading afternoon sun. He'd checked every inch of her during their long shower, pleased none of the lash marks from his flogger were visible. The restaurant where they'd be having dinner catered to people in the lifestyle, and he'd known the dress was going to rattle her—no need to add concern about marks to the mix.

"My happiness... but... why would you think this handkerchief would make me happy? If I sneeze, everybody is going to see so much more of me than they need to. And that's not even mentioning, the odds of my boobs making a surprise appearance are upward of ninety percent. I'll be lucky if I don't get arrested. Good night, nurse, can you imagine the hospital gossip if that happened?"

It was time to shut down her hissy before she said something he'd have to address in a more aggressive way.

"I've asked you to trust me to know what you need, and I've reminded you that needs and wants do not always run parallel." He waited a few beats before continuing. Israel was learning Bristol processed information at warp speed unless it was about her—then it took her a bit longer to internalize anything he tried to tell her. "Jeopardizing your reputation isn't something I would ever do."

He doubted she'd ever been to *The Capriccio*. The up-scale establishment, whose name literally meant *kink* in Italian, wasn't the sort of place anyone watching their budget would go for a casual dinner, nor was it an establishment a submissive would enter alone—the maître d' would politely arrange reservations at a nearby eatery.

"Our dinner reservations are at a specific kind of establishment. It's likely you'll be the most conservatively dressed sub in attendance." Tossing the hanger aside, Israel lifted the dress over her head. "Arms up or use your safe word." After the briefest hesitation, Bristol raised her arms, letting him slip the garment into place. Stepping back, he didn't try to hide his reaction. "Fucking gorgeous. I knew the color would match your eyes." Nodding to the shoes he'd set out for her, he saw her eyes glaze with fear. *What the hell?* She'd objected to the dress but hadn't looked frightened.

"I... I..." Bristol's shoulders dropped, making her look like a deflating balloon. "They're beautiful, but I don't dare wear them. I'm a klutz in sneakers, holy trip over the lines on a basketball court... I'll embarrass us both if I try to walk in those shoes." He watched as she looked longingly at the heels, he could hardly wait to see on her delicate feet.

"I'm going to be right beside you, and this will give me the perfect excuse to keep my hands on you until we're seated. You already know you'll be barefoot once we enter the club, so I want you to give it a try." He smiled when she nodded.

"They're really beautiful, but I'd like to put on panties first, so I don't snag them on the heels." When he shook his head, her eyes widened. "You can't be serious. Look at how short this dress is."

"Think of it as a lesson in perfect posture. Put on the shoes, then I have a gift for you." He knelt in front of her to help slip the shoes into place and smiled up at her once they were in place. "The view from down here is fucking spectacular, baby. If our reservations weren't in half an hour, I'd lick those glistening folds until you came all over my tongue."

If he started something now, they would miss dinner and their trip to the club. Standing slowly, Israel let his gaze move in a heated caress over every delectable curve. Turning her to face the mirror, Israel pulled a slender velvet box from the dresser. Lifting the sapphire and diamond choker, he was pleased to hear her soft gasp.

"Is this one of Catalina's creations? I've heard she is one of the most sought-after jewelry designers in the world."

"It is, and you're right, she is very gifted." Wrapping his arms around her, Israel held the piece where she could see the latch. "This is special for a couple of reasons. First, it will keep you safe at the restaurant and club. It isn't a permanent collar—I'd like to have a more formal ceremony for that occasion when you're ready. This collar will serve three functions tonight. It lets other Doms know you are not available for them to approach. It's also going to look amazing nestled in the hollow of your throat. And finally, it has a built-in safety feature. This is a unique piece, a prototype, a collaboration between Ian McGregor and Catalina."

Not surprisingly, he saw recognition in her eyes when he mentioned Ian's name. Anyone as gifted as Bristol would have enormous respect for someone whose mind was a match for their own. Hell, London thought Ian walked on water. Everyone cleared the room when the two of them started bouncing ideas around.

"I have the only key for the clasp—exactly what everyone familiar with the lifestyle will expect. What they won't know is this lovely piece of jewelry is protecting someone far more precious than the stones around her beautiful neck. No one can steal it—the titanium will keep it in place. An alarm is activated biometrically. You press your fingers to any two sides of the latch for more than two seconds, and it will send out an alarm. The message will go to my phone, Adler Investigations, Cooper Hicks, Catalina and Austin, Kent and Kyle West, Ian McGregor, and Brooklyn's husband, Luke Grayson." It would also monitor her physical reactions and send out an alarm if it detected fear or extreme pain.

"That's a lot of people. Why so many, and what sort of information will they get?"

"We'll immediately know your location and be able to hear you and anyone nearby. We won't be able to communicate with you, but we'll hear everything, so you'd need to feed us information. The name of the person threatening you, whether they are armed, anything that will help." He knew he was scaring her, but he wanted her to understand his concern for her safety.

"Don't you think this is overkill? Someone broke into my apartment. I don't like it either, but this…" She looked down at the choker and frowned. "Why would anyone want to hurt me? Do you really believe a jealous woman would go to this extreme? What happens if I shift? Will I be strangled by the device that's supposed to protect me?"

He hadn't expected this would be easy; she was much too intelligent to simply submit without asking questions. This was probably only the tip of the iceberg.

"That is part of what makes it so special. The damned thing will sense the shift in your DNA and expand and contract as necessary. Devices like these have never been available for shifters, so this is a game-changer. I know you weren't raised in our world, but I assure you, we're very protective of what we feel belongs to us, and we'll spare no expense to keep our mates safe."

Looking from the piece in his hands to meet Bristol's gaze in the mirror, Israel raised a brow, knowing she would understand the unspoken request for permission to lock it in place. At her nod, he snapped the small lock. There was only one key, a small titanium object that looked more like a Greek letter than a device to unlock a choker.

"It's beautiful, and I appreciate Catalina letting me wear it." He smiled and shook his head.

"Bristol, this is a gift. It's probably selfish, but I love seeing something I picked out and bought for you nestled against your ivory skin." He intended to spoil her in every way possible. The two of them wouldn't always have the luxury of a lot of time to spend together, so they'd have to make it a priority, but it would be worth it.

Israel listened carefully as her mind worked through the implications of receiving what was obviously, an extremely valuable gift. He was grateful she moved quickly past any concern he was paying her for sex—the consequences for those questions would have kept them from keeping their reservations. The most amusing part of her internal dialogue was the underlying frustration with herself. Bristol didn't want to want him, but she did. She argued with herself about falling in love when she'd promised herself nothing more than a few rounds of mind-blowing sex before she walked away.

He was winning her over with unrelenting patience, coupled with subtle but loving gestures. Cupping her shoulders, Israel gently turned Bristol until she was facing him.

"Remember, activate the alarm if you are frightened or find yourself face to face with danger." Tunneling his fingers into the long waves of her hair, Israel sealed his lips over hers. A gentle exploration ramped up so quickly, it was torture to pull back.

"Let's go while I still have enough control to keep from tossing you on the bed and burying myself in your hot depths."

Chapter Fourteen

B RISTOL WAS TORN between wanting the car ride to the restaurant to end and wishing they were driving to another state. When Israel had opened the car door for her, Bristol was surprised to find a plush towel folded on her seat. She was even more surprised when he'd told her to lift the back of her dress as he helped her settle on the seat. Leaning across her to secure the seat belt, he'd brushed his lips over hers before pulling back.

"As soon as the door closes, spread your legs and pull the hem of your dress up, so your pussy is available for my touch."

Already reeling from the strange sensation of having her bare ass cheeks against the towel-covered leather seat, it had taken her a few seconds to process the commands. He nodded his approval when he sat next to her, snapping his own seat belt into place without taking his eyes off her bare pussy.

"I love the smell of leather seats, but the aroma of your juices is quickly becoming my favorite scent. I'm going to slip my fingers through those glistening folds, mate. What will I find? Are you wet for me?"

Was that a rhetorical question? He had to know she was

soaked. Her mind cycled quickly through everything she'd learned in her training as a submissive, coming to the realization, a good Dom never asks a question he doesn't want answered, and there was no question in her mind Israel was a good Dom. They may not have been together for a long time, but some things were intuitive.

"Yes, I'm very wet, Sir."

"All those thoughts racing through your mind, lightning doesn't move that fast. You are remarkable." His fingers traced a line of fire up the inside of her thigh, the slow stroke ripe with anticipation. It didn't matter the streetlights were shining down on her bare sex, or the car was so low, it would have been easy for anyone in a higher profile vehicle to look down and see what Israel was doing.

She heard the sucking sound of her juices moving around his fingers as they slipped inside her and felt herself stiffen. It was mortifying to realize her body was so wanton. His low growl shifted her attention to his face. The crinkled line between his brows let her know he wasn't pleased.

"Don't you dare be embarrassed by something I find hotter than hell. Knowing I have this effect on you makes my soul sing and my cock so hard, it's threatening to split open."

She took a deep breath and nodded. His words were empowering. The Dom instructors at the club had continually reminded them, the power was in their hands. Knowing Israel could only command her if she allowed it, Bristol took another long breath and relished the surge of energy, knowing he was turned on by her body's reaction to him.

By the time they pulled into the parking lot beside the exclusive eatery, Bristol's body was begging for release. When she reached for the door handle, Israel leveled a glare at her.

"Stay where you are, Beautiful. Chivalry is not dead in my family. I'd prefer my parents didn't come back to haunt me for letting my mate open her own door." He was around the car in seconds, smiling when he saw she'd pulled the bottom of her dress back into place. Helping her from the low seat, Israel pinned her in, pressing her against the side of the car to take her mouth with a kiss so scorching, he felt the heat radiating around their bodies. When he wrapped his hand around her wrist and pulled her away from the side of the car, Israel pressed his palm against the shiny black metal.

"You're so fucking hot, I can feel it on the surface of the car. Let's go inside. We'll enjoy a nice dinner, then go to Prairie Winds and play."

Bristol zombie walked beside Israel into the restaurant, her head still fogged with lust. The man could kiss her senseless so quickly, it was frightening. In seconds, he could numb enough brain cells to send her IQ down several points.

The small café's entry looked like an open-air terrace, but she'd seen a glimmer of reflection off the pristine glass dome and wondered how many people were fooled by the illusion. There were so many twinkling lights in the surrounding potted trees and plants. One side was a natural stone wall, Bristol suspected was part of some original Austin old west building, making her wonder about the history of the area.

"The owner will be happy to tell you all about the building another time, Beautiful. Tonight is for something entirely different."

They were seated at one of the smaller secluded booths along the rock wall she'd admired when they first arrived. Weaving their way through the tables hadn't been difficult since the establishment wasn't particularly large, but it seemed to take forever because some of the things she'd seen along the way, rendered her mute.

"I had no idea a place like this existed in Austin. Do you come here often?" Bristol hadn't meant for the question to sound insecure, but it was impossible to hide how out of her element she felt.

ISRAEL RECOGNIZED A make-or-break moment when confronted with one, and this one was full of landmines. He wouldn't lie to her, his mate deserved better from him, but he wouldn't let her make more of this than she should.

"I've been here several times, helping friends train subs, group outings, play parties, and an occasional date. Keep in mind, I'm several years older than you, so by default, I'd have more sexual experience. I wasn't a slouch in school, but my parents had their hands full, keeping ahead of London. The rest of us had fairly normal school experiences, so it stands to reason, I had more free time to explore my sexuality." Israel wanted to roll his eyes. Hell, thinking about his behavior was cringeworthy. He'd explored every nook and cranny of his sexual side while dating most of the girls on campus.

"So, you've been here with other women? Dates? I may not have dated in college or a lot after I moved to Texas, but even I know it will be difficult for you to keep from comparing your experiences with other women at this venue. You didn't sit at this table, did you? Holy popping capillaries, maybe we could go through a drive-through and pick up food. You know, eat in the car on the way... Oh... ewww. No other woman has..."

Israel had heard enough. Raising his hand in the universal sign to halt, he shook his head in frustration.

"Stop. I want you to take a breath and listen. Listen very closely, Bristol, because I'm only going to tell you this once." He knew why she was upset but doubted she did. As a group, shifters were notoriously possessive, often displaying inappropriate jealousy during the early stages of the mating process. Bristol hadn't been raised in a shifter household, so she didn't fully understand her feelings.

His mate's emotions had run so hot and cold, he'd barely been able to track them. It was almost painful to watch as her emotions began spiraling into an emotional freefall, knowing she'd been helpless to control the unfamiliar feelings. Signaling the waiter to bring their drinks, he waited until she'd had several sips of wine before proceeding.

"First, I won't lie to you, Bristol. You asked me if I'd been here, and I answered you truthfully. You failed to ask if I've ever been here with a woman I had any interest in claiming as my own, either as a wife or mate. My entire world shifted on its axis when I found you at Kensington and Denali's wedding."

The day had been spectacular. The Adlers celebrated

the marriage of the movie star brother, they'd worried would never find a woman willing to share his insane travel schedule, and Austin's wife, Charlotte, had conveniently forgotten to mention she was in labor, convinced she'd be back in their penthouse apartment before anyone was the wiser.

"I'd have recognized your scent anywhere and known you belonged to me, but having fate bring you into my life on a day when my entire family was present and already celebrating was the icing on the cake. I'd never seat you in a booth or car where anyone—a date or otherwise—had been." Bronx made certain his siblings traded cars regularly, citing some lame-ass excuse about poor advertising when they drove cars more than a year old.

"Ummm... do me a favor and don't tell Bronx about my car, okay?"

He smiled at Bristol. He'd forgotten she could hear him in unguarded moments. Israel was sure his heart had expanded like the damned Grinch—the intimacy of telepathic communication strengthened the bond between mates.

"I won't tell him, but I'd be surprised if he doesn't already know. Austin sent someone to retrieve your car while you were finishing things up with Charlotte. He wanted to make your life easier after you'd ridden in the ambulance to monitor his wife and child. I know I've mentioned this already, but it bears repeating. The Adlers are very protective of our family members. Austin was mortified when a member of his security detail sent pictures of your car."

Israel wasn't enjoying this conversation. The bright red

blush of embarrassment spreading over her cheeks wasn't how he'd intended to start dinner, but on the plus side, she was distracted from her earlier concerns.

"How were they going to bring the car without... oh, wait. I gave you the keys to get my bag, and you didn't have a chance to return them. Geez, I completely forgot to ask for the keys."

"Don't look so shocked, sweetness. I'm damned happy you've been too distracted to think about car keys because that means I'm doing something right."

"You're doing too much right, that's the problem." The words were barely audible, but he hadn't missed them.

"Your car has been secured at one of Bronx's dealerships. Don't worry about having something to drive. Bronx likes you. I can't imagine what sort of sassy car he finds to replace the one he claims was offensive on every level, including various safety issues."

"Oh, dear Goddess. I can't afford a better car. I have another appointment with the architect. He's already asking for more money and hasn't made any of the changes I've asked for. Frickadilly circus, I should have listened to Cam and CeCe. They recommended a firm, but it was out of my price range."

Israel suspected it would have been cheaper for her if she'd hired the more expensive architectural firm. The one she was using underbid and now felt he could hold her hostage by milking every change and charging a huge fee to finish things up.

"The wonderful thing about hindsight, it's twenty-twenty. I'd like for you to talk to Asia about this, Beautiful."

"I don't want to take advantage of your sister, Israel. It would be unfair of me to weasel professional services from her because we are... well, we're..."

"Be very careful how you describe our relationship, my brilliant and beautiful *mate*." Their waiter's arrival with their dinner was fortunate for Bristol. The young man probably saved her a long session over Israel's knee. He'd have given her a few stinging swats now and finished the punishment at the club, but the interruption gave her time to consider her answer and its consequences.

The smile of thanks she gave the other man sent a pang of jealousy racing through Israel's blood before he pulled himself back from the emotion to watch the interaction with an open mind.

"It's nice to see you, Marco. I didn't know you'd taken a second job. How are things with your family? Anything I need to know about?"

"Dr. Banks, it's nice to see you. My family is wonderful, and the twins are growing like weeds. Tuition went up a lot this year, so I'm trying to make up the difference by working here in the evening, but I miss seeing my wife and daughters. I still have several semesters left before I can start my internship, so I need to build up a bit of cushion since my application for assistance with..." The man's nervous glance in Israel's direction spoke volumes.

Decisions on Adler education grant applications had been put on hold recently due to the overwhelming changes taking place within the family. Seeing firsthand how those delays were affecting real people made Israel determined to set the process in motion again on Monday.

"Marco, I want you to call my office first thing Monday

morning." Handing the man one of his business cards, Israel gave him a warm smile. "My assistant, Geneva, will be waiting to help you through whatever obstacles you've encountered."

"Thank you, Mr. Adler." His expression changed from stunned disbelief to gratitude before his eyes became glassy with unshed tears. "Thank you so much." Backing away, excitement vibrating all around him, he nearly tripped over his own feet in his haste. "Enjoy your meal. Please press the button on the table when you're ready for dessert—or if you need anything... anything at all." When he was gone, Bristol turned to him, her expression completely different from anything he'd seen before.

"Thank you. That was very kind. He's very deserving and will be a wonderful physician's assistant. They'd only been married a few weeks when they found out they had twins on the way. His lovely wife was a registered nurse, working in one of the city's larger trauma units, but she had to quit early in her pregnancy. Her job is difficult under normal circumstances, but it was impossible for her to keep up with the physical demands when her body was busy building two tiny humans."

Israel leaned his head back and laughed. He'd had a laundry list of things he wanted to try during dinner, and so far, they hadn't hit a single target. Shaking his head, the irony was more than he could wrap his head around.

"You are full of surprises, Bristol. I had all these kinky things planned, and all my meticulous preparations have been blown out of the water because my date is one of the kindest women I've ever met." The pink tinge of embarrassment, painting her cheeks spoke to her humility, another trait he admired.

"I'm a physician, I'm supposed to be kind."

"You are expected to be professional and compassionate, but I think kindness is something much more basic. Being kind to your fellow human beings isn't always an innate trait, and when you meet someone who is good all the way to the depths of their soul, you've found something extraordinary, indeed."

"Thank you, I'm not sure I've ever received a compliment I appreciated more."

The next few minutes were spent enjoying their steaks. The small restaurant might be best known for kink, but the food was spectacular as well. Beef so tender it melted in your mouth paired with twice-baked potatoes wouldn't weigh them down for what he had planned at the club.

"Before we finish our dinner, I want to give you a little taste of what I had planned." Her hand froze midway between her plate and her luscious lips. Perfect. He had her full attention, and that was exactly what he'd intended. Nodding to her fork, he watched her move it slowly to her mouth, lips parting in anticipation, breath catching with barely banked desire.

"Open those pretty thighs for me, Beautiful, I want to play a bit while you finish eating." Seeing her eyes dilate made his cock jerk against his zipper. The damned thing seemed to have grown a mind of its own since he'd found his mate. Inhaling a deep breath, Israel's senses were bombarded with her scent.

"Fuck me, baby, you are so perfect, I can barely believe my good fortune. I'm not sure what I could have possibly done to deserve you, but I'm not going to question fate's gift." Taking her hand in his, Israel move it back to her plate. "Finish your dinner, sweetness—you're going to need it. You'll be burning up a lot of calories later, and I want to make certain you're properly energized." There was a wealth of meaning in what he said—let her make of it what she would.

When her leg brushed against his, Israel lifted it over his own, so she'd be completely open to his touch. Skimming the pads of his fingers over the sensitive skin on the inside of her thighs, he smiled when goosebumps raced ahead of his caress. The first brush of his fingertips over the slick folds of her sex made him wonder if he'd made a mistake, starting before they were at the club. The restaurant didn't have a policy against public sex, but Israel didn't feel Bristol was ready for that much exposure... *yet*.

The folds were swollen and soaked. It was easy to slide two fingers deep enough to press against her G-spot. Her reaction was everything he'd hoped and more. The quick clench of her vaginal muscles, a heartbeat before a pulse of silky cream warmed the two fingers he'd pushed inside her, was what Doms dreamed of. Leaning close, Israel closed his teeth over the lobe of her ear with enough force to remind her he was in control.

"Come for me, Beautiful," he whispered through clenched teeth.

Her fork clattered to her plate, drawing smiles from several of the patrons. Biting down on her knuckle to stifle her scream, the sound she made was music to his ears—the whimper perfect. Bristol's release had been little more than a pop-off valve, letting off a bit of steam. It wasn't the bone-melting orgasm her body was chasing, but he hadn't intended for it to be more than a temporary reprieve.

Israel paid the check, slipping several one-hundred-dollar bills into the tip portion of the folder. It wasn't much, but he suspected the young family would be grateful for any help they received. Setting the folder on the table, he looked up to see Bristol watching him, her eyes brimming unshed tears made his breath catch. What the hell?

"Bristol, what's wrong? Are you ill?"

She shocked him when she fisted her small hands in the front of his shirt and pulled him close. Sealing her lips over his, the kiss ramped up like a flash fire. Israel couldn't remember the last time he'd allowed a woman to take the lead and was shocked at how much he'd enjoyed feeling her need wash over him.

"Nothing. Nothing at all. That money will mean so much to them. His wife won't be cleared to return to work for another three weeks." She brushed away an errant tear and smiled. "I... well, I just wanted to say thank you. I didn't understand the importance of planting trees that I would never have the opportunity to sit under until I was taken in by a loving teacher after my parents died. She taught me more in the short time I was with her than my parents had in all the years I'd spent living in their house."

The significance of Bristol's words wasn't lost on him. Who the hell referred to their childhood as the years they spent living in their parents' house? Pushing his anger on her behalf aside, Israel pulled her into his arms.

"I want you to promise to help Asia with the foundation education programs. You know as well as any of us how important it is." Without giving her a chance to turn down his request, Israel grasped her hand and led her to the car.

Even in the dim light, Israel could see her eyes widen in surprise when he led her to a Lincoln Town Car. The driver, one of his company's more seasoned employees, Lincoln Billings, was also the first member of the security team Israel was putting together for Bristol. Lincoln opened the back door, giving them both a polite nod.

"Good evening, Dr. Banks, Mr. Adler."

Bristol stopped so quickly, Israel nearly ran over her. He hadn't planned to introduce them until they were safely inside the car, but it seemed she had other ideas. Bristol extended her hand in greeting.

Chapter Fifteen

I T DIDN'T TAKE a rocket scientist to figure out what Israel had planned for them during the drive to the club outside town. It wasn't a long trip, but with the city's growing population moving farther and farther outside the perimeter of Austin, traffic was becoming more challenging. The car was luxurious, but it wasn't particularly private. There was an added layer of tension pulsing beneath the surface when she'd stopped to introduce herself to the man who'd greeted her, making her wonder what she wasn't being told.

"So many worries bouncing around inside your pretty head, let's see if we can't find something else for you to focus on. Untie the halter of your dress and lower the front, so your breasts are fully exposed, Bristol." Israel didn't expect her to comply without some hesitance. She was in a car with a man she didn't know and sitting next to a window as they passed under streetlights as they slowly made their way out of the city. Bristol took a deep breath, then released it before reaching for the loose knot at the top of her back. She saw surprise reflected in Israel's intense gaze and knowing he'd misjudged her was empowering.

When Bristol shook Lincoln Billings' hand, she'd known instantly he was a shifter. His intensity, posture, and attentive nature made her think he was also a Dom. There was no reason to ask questions when she already knew the answer. Israel had already told her he enjoyed exhibition, and she was smart enough to recognize a test when she encountered one. When she finally worked the knot free, Bristol took another deep breath, hoping the added oxygen would fuel her courage. The two sides dropped to her lap, and the cool air from the car's ventilation system kissed her nipples, making them draw into tight peaks.

"You have spectacular breasts, baby. Pale ivory skin and cotton candy pink nipples that are so responsive, they make me want to weep with gratitude." When they stopped at for a red light, Israel grinned. "What do you think, Linc? Doesn't my mate have beautiful breasts?" The driver gave her a considering look over his right shoulder, laser-focused on her nipples before his appreciative gaze moved up to her face.

"They are gorgeous, but I think they might be eclipsed by those high cheekbones and halo of blonde silk. I'm a sucker for both."

Bristol felt warmth spread over her cheeks at his compliment and appreciated him shifting his attention away from her breasts. He was a Dom, but it was obvious, he didn't see that as his role in her life. Tobi had tried to explain this concept to her a few months after Bristol joined Prairie Winds, but it hadn't made sense until now.

"Don't get all creeped out when your Dom wants to show off what belongs to him. I swear they are all a bunch of junior high school boys at heart. In a weird way, it's like waggling their dicks at each other to see who can make it swing the most." Tobi, irreverent goofball they all loved, emphasized her point with a series of hip gyrations, sending the other submissives into hysterics. "And if your nipples or clit-hood are pierced? You're going to find yourself sitting on the fireplace mantel, naked as the day you were born, with all your *pretties* displayed for everyone's viewing pleasure."

Tobi's reference to the narrow ledge above the electronic fireplace made Bristol shiver. The native stone piece was a focal point in the room, featuring moveable pegs for the sub's feet, designed to keep a submissive from slipping from the mantelpiece and falling to the floor. Apparently, Doms were creative and loved discovering new ways to place the pegs in their never-ending quest to make certain their sub was perfectly displayed.

A sharp pinch to her nipples pulled Bristol back from her wandering mind. When she tried to lift her hands in a futile effort to shield the throbbing nubs, she realized Israel had easily shackled her wrists in his large hands, pinning them in her lap.

"Wait for it, Beautiful. Wait for the pain to morph into something more—something on the other side of the coin."

Bristol understood the reference, one the Wests often referred to during her training. As a physician, she was programmed to believe, while pain wasn't pleasant, it could be an indication the healing process was beginning. The concept of pain and pleasure being two sides of the same coin had taken a while to wrap her head around.

"I know the submissive training at Prairie Winds is top-notch, but it's only meant to teach you the basics. The Doms want to give you enough information, so you can make informed choices and hopefully, keep you from making any major mistakes in protocol." Kyle West had said essentially the same thing at the beginning and end of the mandatory training. Bristol hadn't made any mistakes because she'd been meticulous during the few evenings she'd been able to visit the club.

Israel's warm mouth surrounded her nipples, his teeth biting down on the stiff tip as he pulled back, elongating the peak. He held up two oddly shaped pieces of metal, and it took Bristol's brain several seconds to kick into gear. *Nipple clamps.* She'd heard subs say their nipples hurt for days after wearing certain types of clamps, but her thoughts were racing too fast to remember which ones were the worst.

"These are very mild, Beautiful. They aren't intended to cause pain—these little beauties will keep your nipples aroused. They'll look like gorgeous flowers under your dress. While I put them on you, I want you to tell me what your safe words are and when you are supposed to use them."

Aww, another test—something she was good at. She'd no sooner started explaining the stoplight system for safe words, reciting the information verbatim, when her entire body felt like it was heating from her core and spreading outward in rolling waves of pleasure. Leaning her head back, Bristol forgot all about being topless in the backseat of a car with a man, she'd only just met, driving them to a club where she would probably be even more exposed than she was now. A needy moan vibrated from her core all the way up her throat until the sound escaped on a slow exhale.

"You are so responsive. If I'd drawn up the plans for my perfect mate and sub, I couldn't have done better. I'm going to thank the great Goddess every day for the rest of my life." He blew puffs of air over the sensitive tips, and Bristol felt the clench all the way to her toes. Her pussy was so wet, she hoped the evidence of her arousal wouldn't slide down the inside of her thighs when she stood. Israel lifted the front of her dress and leaned close to retie the ends.

"If it does, I'll be the cockiest bastard to walk through the doors of the club. Fuck me, that would be hot as hell."

She appreciated his words, even though they didn't do anything to make her worry less. She'd finally gotten her heart and respiration rate under control when they parked in front of the club. Lincoln opened her door, giving her a quick nod before turning to Israel.

"I'll be inside in a few minutes. I want to check for Ms. Williams' car. We have reason to believe she is onsite."

Israel nodded his understanding, his eyes continually scanning the area surrounding the club's impressive entrance. Bristol thought they were overreacting but was wise enough to keep it to herself. After they'd signed in, she hurried along the outside edge of the main room to the hall leading to the women's locker room. Bristol planned to store her shoes in her personal locker and freshen up before rejoining Israel.

The music was cranked up with dancers packed like sardines on the small dance floor. The line dances would

soon give way to pairings, where the moves were decidedly sexier.

Bristol was distracted as she turned the corner into the
short hall leading to the locker rooms, quickly apologizing
when she ran into someone moving so fast, she wouldn't
have been able to identify them if it hadn't been for the
woman's distinctive scent. Why hadn't Clovia Williams
stopped to say hello? *Maybe she was frustrated with you for
walking around with your head up your ass.* Great, now she
was talking to herself.

Walking into the locker room was usually uplifting, the
other women always laughing and joking about something.
They left titles at the door, Dommes and subs all the same
behind the heavy wooden door. Today, Bristol was greeted
by an eerie silence and a sense of foreboding. Tobi, Jen, and
Gracie were standing in a semi-circle, staring at Bristol's
locker. Their arms crossed over breasts barely contained in
the skimpy outfits they were wearing as they focused their
attention on her locker.

"What's going on?" Bristol tried to keep her question
upbeat but knew she hadn't been successful. Even she
could hear the worry in her voice.

"I saw Clovia come in while we were in the sitting
room. She was carrying a burlap bag. It thought it was
weird, but people surprise me all the time."

"I just met her in the hall, and she wasn't carrying anything." The hair on the back of Bristol's neck was standing
on end. She sensed danger but couldn't get a lock on where
it was coming from.

"She was in this area. I heard a padlock being opened
but didn't remember her locker is on the other side of the

room until Gracie mentioned it. When I called out to her, the spooky bitch took off like her tail feathers were on fire."

"Your locker is making a strange sound, Bristol. I called Micah, he should be here in…" The door of the locker room crashed open, the space quickly filling with so many people, Bristol wondered if the entire club was now standing in the ladies' dressing area. Jax McDonald's booming voice startled her as Israel's warm arms pulled her back against his chest, wrapping her in his embrace.

"Come with me, Beautiful. I want you out of here while this is sorted out." His warm breath moved over her ear, making her pink bits tingle.

"What about my friends? I don't want them facing something scary when it wasn't intended for them. I don't understand this. I bumped into Clovia when I came into the hall but didn't realize it was her until it was too late. When I walked in here, everyone was staring at my locker. The whole thing is like some cheesy movie plot… one of those straight-to-video specials in the dollar bin, six months after they're released." She felt his chest vibrate against her back and felt his amusement wash over her. "It's not funny. I worked so hard to build a practice I could be proud of, and somehow, I've landed a starring role in a no-budget nightmare." Israel spun her around so fast, Bristol wobbled in the heels she'd been looking forward to ditching.

"This is not your fault and doesn't reflect on you in any way." Before he could say any more, he frowned at something behind her. Turning back to the group, Bristol was surprised to see Del West with a stethoscope pressed to the front of her locker. His frown told her, he wasn't at all happy with whatever he'd heard.

"Get everybody out and call Animal Control. The ladies were right, it's a *rattling* sound, for sure. Probably several small rattlers, and they're going to be pissed off when the damned locker door is opened."

Bristol felt her knees fold out from under her. *Snakes? Fucking hell in Hollywood. This lame-ass B movie was sinking lower and lower by the minute.* Voices were shouting around her, but thankfully they sounded oddly distant… and why was she floating through the air? *Very odd, indeed.* Reality was fading fast, and she was grateful for the reprieve. Hell, she couldn't have pulled it back if she'd wanted to, and at this rate, she honestly didn't care.

"Let go, Bristol, I've got you." Israel's whispered words were the last thing she heard before the darkness closed in, but she'd never forgotten how wonderful it felt to know someone had her back. The sense of security was unfamiliar, but she pulled it around her heart like a warm blanket.

NOBODY HAD TO tell Tobi twice to vacate the locker room. She looked around the table and shuddered. "I hate snakes. I hate them with a passion most people reserve for thermonuclear war and their husband's ex-girlfriends."

"I don't like them, either, but I'm focusing on the snake who put them in the damned locker. I say we let the guys deal with the slithering kind, and we deal with the snake who ran out of here like a fucking coward." Jen's tone was ice cold, and her words were everything Tobi was thinking. In all the time she'd been at Prairie Winds, Tobi had never seen one club member deliberately endanger another. It was unforgivable. As Kent escorted her out of the locker room, he warned her to stay out of it. The damned man knew her too well.

"We can go hunting, I know where she lives." Tobi and Jen froze, staring at Gracie with their mouths hanging open in shocked silence, they all knew wouldn't last long.

"Damn... I didn't see that coming. Hell, Gracie, I've been worried you were going for sainthood." Tobi's eyes widened, a look of sudden awareness changing her expression from surprise to horror as she shot out of her seat, "Well, frosted Fiddle Faddle."

"You realize our reputations are in tatters, right?" Jen slumped back in her seat, disillusionment easy to see on her pretty face. "Cripes, we've turned into well-behaved subs. It's positively mortifying. How the hell did we let this happen?"

"I don't know. I'm stunned. Lilly always tells me if I'm screwing up—she's the mom I missed so much. I can't believe she didn't tell me I'm boring." Dropping back into her chair, shaking her head in disbelief, Tobi felt shell shocked. "I feel old. We need to have a party. I've become an embarrassment to Lilly—her heart is probably broken. She'd have never introduced a prosaic woman to her sons, let alone allowed them to marry one."

"Kitten, I have no idea where you get these crazy ideas." Kyle West plucked his wife out of the chair with practiced ease. Pulling her against his chest and cupping her ass with his large hands, he claimed her mouth. The kiss, so hot the temperature in the room had to have risen several degrees, wiped all the consternation from her mind. Tobi lost herself in the pleasure her husbands always brought. Every kiss, every touch, every whispered endearment set her body and soul on fire—as potent today as they'd been when she first met them.

Kyle had almost run over her when the piece of shit car she'd been driving to interview them became disabled on the side of the highway during a thunderstorm. The electricity had been so strong between them, it overshadowed the lightning bolts outside his truck as he'd driven her to his home. Kent met them in the parking garage a few minutes later, and she'd been helpless to resist his charms. The brothers' personalities were actually quite similar, but their unique communication styles made them appear more different than she knew they were.

When Kyle finally pulled back to look into her eyes, his satisfied smile told her he'd done exactly what he'd intended. "You could never disappoint our mother, Kitten. She adores you and would be shocked to find out you consider it a possibility."

She felt her heart squeeze in regret.

"Sweet Cheeks, you are not boring, although I'll concede the three of you have been awfully well-behaved lately." Jax McDonald shook his head as he shifted his attention from Tobi to his wife. "Cariño, we are going to talk about this sudden desire to misbehave. I suspect there is more to this than we see on the surface—Micah and I want you to know there are better, safer ways to get attention." Tobi watched Gracie's tanned cheeks blush deep rose and hoped their *conversation* wasn't too painful.

"Glad my men are in BFE, chasing baddies. No reason to get them all riled up." Jen probably didn't realize the thread of pain in her voice, but Tobi heard it, and from the look on Kyle's face, he hadn't missed it, either.

"Since I'm the one who sent Sam and Sage to bum-fuck Egypt, I'll be the one to update them on their sub's disillusionment—something I'm sure they are unaware of and will find as disconcerting as the rest of us." Tobi flinched, knowing Kyle's frustration was misplaced. He must have felt her reaction because he pulled in a steadying breath before releasing her and moving to Jen. Pulling her into a quick hug, Kyle pressed a quick kiss against the top of her head and stepped back. "I'm sorry, darlin', that was out of line. The truth is, we've been expecting this." He waved his hand between the three women.

"We hadn't realized how distracted we'd become until recently—then we didn't know what to do about it." Jax looked down at his wife, regret reflecting in his eyes. "The last thing in the entire world any of us wanted was to make you feel was as if you'd lost any of your sparkle. Nothing could be further from the truth."

Tobi watched Jax and Kyle reach for their phones at the same time and groaned. Good news didn't involve conference calls or group texts. Trouble and security issues traveled faster than the speed of light at Prairie Winds. Both men murmured curses vile enough peel wallpaper from the wall before turning their attention back to the women.

"Ladies, please follow us. We're going to use the outside fire escape. You're going to take Tobi's car and go straight to Adler Oil. Asia is setting up a little party for you. One of the security staff will meet you in the underground parking area and escort you upstairs. Israel has already headed that way with Bristol."

"They'll have clothes for you. Enjoy yourselves, and we'll keep Israel posted on things here. Leave your phones here, and do not let anyone know where you are." Jax wasn't usually an alarmist, which made his comments all the more disturbing.

"You don't want someone to track us, using our phones?"

"No, we don't. Your phones won't work inside the building, anyway. Israel's team is scrambling everything, but there's a chance you could be tracked until you pulled into the garage."

"Which is the same as painting a big X on a map." Kyle pushed his hand through his hair in frustration. "No one thinks you were the target, but whoever put eight rattlesnakes in Bristol's locker had no regard for the other people endangered."

"Eight? Oh my God. Did they get them all? Oh shit, you think there are more, don't you? That's why we can't use the elevator." Tobi's knees folded out from under her, but Kyle had been ready. Tossing a set of keys to Jen, Kyle gave her a mock frown.

"It's a car, Jen, not a plane or chopper. Drive safely— yes, we'll be tracking you and will know if you decide to play fast and loose with the rules." He gave Tobi a quick hug before sending them on their way, down the outside stairwell.

"I don't know why you get to drive. It's my car."

"Because you're such a girl, going all weak-kneed over snakes. I don't like them either, but I'd rather die than listen to Sam and Sage rag on my ass about being weak. If I let them know how scared I was of all things slithering, they'd bring home every creepy crawly thing they could find, trying to cure me." Jen shuddered as she unlocked Tobi's Hummer with the remote.

"Buckle up, ladies. Let's see what this beast is made of."

Chapter Sixteen

ISRAEL LEANED BACK in his leather office chair, staring at the row of monitors, and shaking his head in utter frustration. Where the hell did Clovia Williams get fucking rattlesnakes? Hell, he'd run half the damned state in his wolf and could count on one hand the number of times he'd seen a rattler. The young men from Animal Control had been so surprised by the number of reptiles in the locker, they'd let one get away from them. The entire Prairie Winds security team spent hours looking for the damned thing, finally finding it curled around a chandelier over their heads—hiding in plain sight.

"I've been trying to call the Alpha of her pack, but I'm having trouble connecting. I'm going to give him another few hours, then I'll take another route. Charlotte over-heard our conversation about the snakes. I'd bet you rocks, marbles, or chalk she called her Aunt Gigi."

Israel felt his eyes widen. His sister-in-law, Charlotte, was magical royalty. Her grandfather, Audric Stafford, had been the head of the Magical Council for Israel's entire life. Charlotte's mother, Amaya, could control water and wind, and her father, Eamon, was the chief ruler of the bayou, leading a number of different magicals, who'd come together to protect their small territory. But it was Charlotte's aunt, Brigitte Stafford, who was the undisputed star of the family. Gigi was one of the most powerful witches in the western hemisphere, a wild child with a free spirit and a wicked sense of humor, a respected Domme, and a member of kink clubs all over the world.

"I'll let the security team know Brigitte may blow in on the wind. I can't imagine her ignoring Charlotte's call. Expect her to show up, loaded with baby gifts and enough magical ammo to blow Clovia Williams into the next millennium."

Israel smiled to himself, knowing most of the team had either met Charlotte's aunt or heard about her—every man he knew either adored or was terrified of Brigitte. Her presence wasn't going to play out in Clovia's favor. Bristol would be considered under the Stafford family's protection. Charlotte loved her, and Bristol had managed the successful delivery of the highly anticipated new generation of magical aristocracy under difficult conditions.

"I love Gigi, but you and I both know she isn't going to take this well." Austin nodded his head toward the monitor, showing the women gathered around the pool, drinks in hand. "Most of them have been hitting the sauce for an hour. They're going to throw Nurse Ratched under the bus in thirty seconds or less. We may be having trouble locating her, but Brigitte won't."

"I'd like to interview her before the Council gets their shot. It's important to confirm she was the only one involved. For all we know, she wasn't acting alone. If there are other players, we need to know who they are." Israel didn't think there were, but he wasn't willing to bet

Bristol's or anyone else's life on it. Returning his gaze to the monitor focused on the table where the women were holding court, he smiled affectionately at Charlotte.

"I'm glad to see Charlotte joining them. Girl time might not be as physically restorative as sleep, but from the smile on her face, I'd say it's feeding her soul." Israel turned to his oldest brother when he didn't respond and found him staring transfixed on the screen.

"When I married her, I didn't think I could love her any more than I did at that moment. I was wrong." Austin had dated infrequently after inheriting the CEO position—he hadn't had time. His work schedule had been grueling, and he'd spent many nights in the bedroom hidden behind his office suite. "She was the best executive assistant I've ever had. Everyone in the office begged me to find another wife, so they could keep her at work." Austin chuckled and shook his head. "I was called a selfish oaf more often than I care to recount."

"The irony is most of those working on your floor are shifters and know exactly how mating works." Israel couldn't hold back his laughter. It said a lot about how much everyone loved Charlotte if they'd been willing to risk yanking the boss's chain to keep her in the office.

"I miss having her there, but I'm thrilled she wants to spend this time with our son. Hell, I wouldn't get anything done if she was there."

Israel was sure that much was true. He could see himself spending every waking minute inside Bristol if they worked together. Austin's shoulders seemed to relax, his smile making Israel wonder what he was thinking.

"I didn't read all the books everyone sent me. A few

days into the great book barrage, as Charlotte referred to it. I figured out what you asshats were up to, so I chose wisely, as the old knight told Indiana Jones. I might not have gotten through them all, but I got through enough to understand how important the bonding time is for both of them." Austin flashed him an unrepentant grin, making Israel laugh again.

"There was some heavy betting on who could come up with the best book. Everybody wants the bragging rights for getting you to read theirs. Let us know what you read and in what order." There was no question Austin would remember—the man probably remembered what he wore to school the first day of fucking third grade.

"I'm the luckiest bastard alive. My wife is brilliant, submissive with enough sass to keep me on my toes, and—"

"*And that is definitely* more information than I needed." Brigitte shimmered into view beside Austin, giving him a quick hip check in greeting. "Fill me in. What the fuck is this about snakes at the club? I'll bet that sent Kyle into orbit. Since I've heard she's a shifter, I'm calling first dibs on whoever is responsible. The Wests can have whatever's left." Brigitte gave them both a cheeky grin. Damn witch already knew he didn't want her getting the first shot—there wasn't a chance in hell there'd be anything left for the rest of them to deal with.

Austin gave her a quick overview of everything that had happened since they'd left the house to go to Kensington's wedding. No doubt he wanted to reinforce how important Dr. Bristol Banks was to not only Charlotte, but Israel as well.

"I'm not surprised Charlotte didn't tell anyone she was

in labor. She never seems to remember how special she is or how quickly her body heals." She shrugged before adding, "It's going to be interesting to see how quickly Marshall's magic develops. You should probably count on sooner rather than later." When she finished, Gigi looked at Israel.

"Dr. Banks belongs to you?" When he nodded, she rolled her eyes in an overly dramatic display of frustration. "I suppose this means you're going to want in on the takedown, then talk her to death before I whisk her away to appear before the Council of Magic."

"Yes, I'd like to interview her, Brigitte."

"Semantics, my dear. It's all about semantics." Looking at the screen, Brigitte watched her beloved niece throw her head back in easy laughter. Gigi's expression softened. "You're good for her, Austin. I've never seen her this happy and relaxed. Her parents put a lot of pressure on her to keep their little corner of the world safe from Adler Oil. She fought coming, feeling like she was being prostituted for the good of the bayou, but her deeply ingrained sense of loyalty to her family and friends finally won."

"I'm damned glad. I can't imagine my life without her. If you want to spend time with her, you better get a move on—I can see she's fading fast from here."

"Places to go, people to see, babies to spoil, bitches to toast." With a quick flick of her wrist, Brigitte Stafford disappeared in a cloud of pink smoke.

"Drama Queen." Austin rolled his eyes and chuckled.

"I heard that." Gigi's disembodied voice pinged around the room. Israel shook his head and chuckled.

"It's easy to see why Charlotte loves her. Hell, I wish

she was my aunt."

"What she said about Marshall makes me wonder what we might be up against. Goddess knows, his gene pool is off the damn chart." Austin's worried expression was damned amusing since his son was only a couple of days old. His phone chimed with an incoming message. Skimming it, Israel looked at his brother.

"Let's go. They've found a condo in a name traced to Clovia Williams. It's across the fucking street. She has a bird's-eye view into my suite. Date of sale—six months after the only scene I ever did with her and two months after I stopped trying to explain we weren't fated mates."

"Doesn't sound like she took you seriously."

BRISTOL TRIED TO concentrate on the conversation taking place in Israel's office, but telepathic communication from this distance wasn't easy for her, and the antics of the women surrounding her made them nearly impossible to ignore.

"We needed Lilly. She once shot a snake to smithereens to protect a guy she didn't even like. She'd have had a heyday shooting up the locker room."

"She'd have needed a cannon... not to say she would be opposed to a cannon. Now that I think about it, she'd probably leap at the chance." Gracie giggled, taking another gulp of the drink Asia set in front of her a few minutes ago.

The second oldest Adler elected herself as the group's bartender, claiming since the entire space had been her idea, it was her duty to act as hostess. "And... I know where all the good booze is hidden."

"I'm not sure whether we should be horrified or impressed. I don't know anyone brave enough to gather that many rattlesnakes. That bitch is nuts." Jen's entire body shuddered at the thought.

"Does Israel have a lot of women in his past?" Bristol hadn't intended to ask the question aloud, but now that the words slipped out, she might as well jump in with both feet. "What I mean is... would this be an ongoing problem for anyone to have a relationship with him?"

"Just as well take the question out of that relationship comment, sister. Hell, Helen Keller could see that's a done deal." One of the things Bristol loved about Tobi was her cut-to-the-chase communication style. Tobi and Gracie had built a thriving consulting business after their Forum Shops idea made the Prairie Winds Club, not only one of the most respected kink clubs in the country but also one of the most lucrative. Bristol felt herself blush at Tobi's comment.

"Tobi's right. I don't think I've ever seen Master Israel look at a woman the way he does you." Gracie took a drink from her margarita and sighed. "I bet God wondered why it took humans so long to figure out why he made limes." Giggling, she drained her glass and shrugged when she looked surprised it was empty. "I've watched him do flogging scenes, and there's a reason he is so popular, not only as a Dom but also as an instructor. It's like he can read the submissive's mind—his focus is legendary." *If you only knew. I've never known anyone who could read someone's thoughts as easily as Israel Adler.* "He swept into the locker room like a damned hurricane, zeroed in on you without looking at anyone else."

"Yeah, Rattler Rita could have set herself on fire naked, and he wouldn't have given her a second glance. I'd like to get my hands around that bitch's throat. I hate fucking snakes. When I was in Costa Rica, there were snakes everywhere. People just accepted it—what's up with that? I set off the panic alarm in my office when I found a snake curled up under my desk, and the locals thought I'd lost my mind." Jen's left-of-center sense of humor was gas to Tobi's fire. Everyone who knew them enjoyed the way they played off one another.

"Why didn't you shoot it? Didn't they give you a gun? Why would our government send you to a country with snakes without a gun? That shit's covered in the Bill of Rights. Something about no cruel and unusual punishment... wait, are you covered by that if you're out of the country? You should be if you're working for the government. Hey, Asia... we have a legal conun... um... condum... shit... question."

Asia didn't bother responding to Tobi's tirade. She probably knew it was pointless since most of them would forget the question in a few minutes, anyway.

"First of all, the asshole who sent me there was probably hoping I'd be eaten by a snake. Don't forget, some snakes have two legs. Fucking hell, there's something I never thought I say." The women all giggled, the alcohol definitely taking effect. Most of the tension had been replaced by more relaxed emotions.

"I agree, Jen. Snakes give me the creeps, and I've seen too many of them for my peace of mind."

Bristol placed her hand on Catalina's forearm, the gesture meant to comfort, but she felt an entirely different sensation—like being sucked into a swirl of brilliant color, then dropped into a barren, concrete block cell with dirt floors. Of all the sensations assailing her senses, it was the stench of death that was the worst. One of the reasons she'd chosen her specialty was the lower incidence of death. Her rotations in the emergency, geriatric, and cancer wards had nearly broken her spirit.

Negativity bombarded her from all sides, and in the distance, she heard a woman whimper. Before she could follow the sound, Bristol was being pulled back through the tunnel. This time, the colors in the tunnel weren't as brilliant, but the air was charged in a way she couldn't describe. Blinking back her confusion, Bristol looked around at her friend's concerned expressions.

"Have you ever had a DNA test, Bristol?" Confused, Bristol looked up at a woman she'd never seen before.

"Aunt Gigi, let her get her bearings before you delve into her genome. Bristol is brilliant, but even her mind has to reset after... well, after whatever that was. Don't ask me hard questions, I just had a baby, and I swear he took several IQ points with him when he was born."

"I hear ya, sister. I felt like the village idiot for months after the twins were born. It was depressing as hell. And that wasn't even counting the traumatic experience of walking past a mirror."

Bristol was finally getting her emotional footing. At least they were talking about a subject she had an academic understanding of—whatever she'd experienced, touching Catalina Adler was something else entirely.

"I had the same problem with mirrors. Those fuckers were my worst enemy." Tobi and Jen stared at Gracie as if she'd grown a new head, but the beautiful Latina continued on, undeterred. "I had the perfect solution to the mirror problem, too. I covered them with blankets. You'd have thought I committed some heinous crime against humanity. My men went ballistic, tearing down all the blankets and, in general, making my life hell. I kept all my responses in rapid-fire Spanish in self-defense."

"I thought they learned Spanish, so they knew when you were cursing at them?"

"They did, but I have dialects, slang, and speed on my side. Total beginners mistake on their part." Every woman at the table burst into laughter at Gracie's uncharacteristic snark.

"Focus, ladies. Great Goddess, what's a witch have to do to get a drink around here? It seems I need to catch up." Brigitte turned to Asia. "Would you mind making me a frozen margarita with extra everything?"

"On it." Asia flashed the woman a smile before moving down the glossy wood bar to fill the woman's drink order.

"I'm Brigitte Stanford, Dr. Banks, and I'm very happy to meet you. On behalf of my entire family, I'd like to thank you for what you did for Charlotte. Bringing Marshall safely into the world isn't something we'll ever forget... and we take care of our own."

Jen leaned closer to Charlotte in a move so overly dramatic, it was almost comical, asking in the loudest stage whisper Bristol had ever heard, "Is she really a witch?" When Charlotte nodded, Jen whistled. "Fucking spectacular. I swear to all things holy, Betty would have loved you all." When they gave her a quizzical look, the pretty blonde shrugged. "My neighbor in D.C. She was a spy. Her life was filled with the most amazing adventures. I like to think of her as the Lilly of the East Coast."

"Nothing scarier than trying to get information from a group of inebriated subs." The woman who'd introduced herself as a witch shook her head in amazement.

"Hey, I resent that. I'm breastfeeding, so no booze for me. Can't have Marshall staggering around the nursery. Austin is probably spying on me, anyway. I swear every time I come up here, I see more cameras. The Adlers are trying to compete with the Wests, raising paranoia to an elite science."

"Your honey is not spying—at least not now. They are on their way across the street, chasing shadows. I could have warned them Clovia Williams isn't there, but they wouldn't have listened—men, what can I say?" Every woman at the table was staring at Charlotte's aunt in awe. She shrugged before taking a long sip of her drink. "I know they'll tell you all about it, so I'll skip the details. I want to talk about what happened to Bristol when she touched Catalina."

Cat shifted in her seat, her gaze seeking the support of her older sister. Asia hadn't missed the cue and stepped behind her. Crossing slender arms over her chest, Asia Adler was in full bad-ass corporate lawyer mode.

"Relax, ladies. I don't want to get into *what* she saw, I'm interested in the process and why she was able to connect without trying. I'll get to Cat later because I'm starting to see a pattern to these connections. This is a situation the Council is watching carefully. There are several possible answers, and knowing it happened to Denali and Bristol raises some interesting questions. On the surface, they appear to be from vastly different backgrounds, but we have information indicating there may be a lot more going on."

Everyone was enthralled with what Brigitte was saying, and Bristol could practically hear the wheels of intelligence spinning all around her.

"I didn't do anything to initiate the connection aside from laying my hand on her forearm. I've never experienced anything like it. My connection to Israel is much different, and this took me by surprise." Bristol needed time to process everything else—the tunnel of swirling color, the desolation and stench of the cell, and the heart-wrenching whimper of an injured woman.

"The Council has traced Denali's family back so far, we ran out of written records and had to resort to…" Brigitte looked around the table and smiled. "Well, let's say we had to use other means. But, you… you are another story. We have full dossiers on the agents who raised you."

"*Agents?* What do you mean, agents? My parents were much too lazy to be agents for anyone."

"The couple we believe were your biological parents died when you were an infant, Bristol. More accurately, they were killed by a shadow agency the Council has been tracking for more than a hundred years. So much of the unrest in the world today has nothing to do with what you see and hear on the news. There is an epic battle between good and evil being waged in the magical community—the energy from the war is spilling over into the non-magical world."

"Holy fucking hell." Asia set her hands on Catalina's shoulders, giving her a reassuring squeeze.

"What we don't know is what it has to do with Catalina, Denali, and Bristol. We have a vast DNA registry. Matching might take a few weeks, but I assure you, we'll find what we're looking for.

"I'd like to make a deal with you, Bristol. I'll solve the problem you're having with the crazy snake bitch—in turn, we'd like your help, unraveling the connection between the three of you."

Tobi leaned forward, locked on Bristol. "They want your blood. Make sure they take it in the traditional manner, and if you see Robert Pattinson... *run*." Charlotte was the first to burst out laughing, followed quickly by the others.

"Your Masters don't beat you enough, Tobi." Brigitte's reprimand was negated by the amusement in her voice. "Bless your non-magical heart. You could at least do me the courtesy of eluding to my being a real vampire rather than some Hollywood pretty boy."

"That pretty boy is worth one hundred million dollars. Evidently, bad acting and a lame script pay remarkably well." Jen leaned back in her chair, rolling her glass on edge, making water circles on the teak tabletop. "I'm curious..."

"Oh shit, here it comes. Jen, the former diplomat, is a tough cookie. Watch and learn, ladies." Tobi's narration sent another wave of giggles around the table, but Jen's focus on Brigitte never wavered.

"Who draws the blood, and who processes it? If Bristol's whole childhood was a lie, why would she believe you now? No one asks for a DNA sample unless they already have a good idea what they are looking for—so, what's your angle?" Catalina and Asia both raised their brows, surprised by Jen's insight. Bristol was impressed with her friend's condensed version of the questions running through her head.

"I wouldn't expect her to believe me without someone speaking on my behalf. Ask Charlotte if I'm trustworthy. Ask her if I work on behalf of the Magic Council. As for who will draw and have access to the blood, it was a concern we anticipated. We'd like you to go to Boston."

"Of course, you mean the Monroe Estate. Israel isn't going to agree to anyone else being involved." Asia's words were barely polite, her voice frosty, but Brigitte was unaffected. "Did you mention this when you spoke with Israel and Austin earlier?" Charlotte's aunt raised a brow at the challenge, but Asia stood her ground.

"No, I didn't say anything to the men, out of respect for Dr. Banks. She is an adult, and aside from a few drinks, I believe she is more than capable of deciding whether to help us make sense of this. I wouldn't have talked to her in front of this group, but I knew there wasn't a chance in hell I could get her alone. Face it, you're a formidable group of women."

"It's okay to tell her you want to think about it, Bristol." Charlotte's soft-spoken words penetrated Bristol's racing thoughts, warming her heart.

"I'm not the enemy here. I'm trying to help you navigate murky waters without getting eaten by sharks. Clovia Williams is well-connected politically. Note, I didn't say she was popular, but she's got an impressive pedigree within the magical community, so you're going to need equal clout to take her down."

"I don't understand what any of this means. I'm sure your offer of help is sincere, but I don't make a decision without fully understanding everything involved." Bristol was starting to feel as though everything was closing in around her. It was suffocating and frightening.

Good girl. We're on our way back. Austin and I want to join your conversation. Hang in there, the Calvary is coming.

Israel's voice moved through her mind, the words bringing a wave of relief. She'd been alone for so long, it was nice to know she had people willing to help her avoid making a mistake. Before she started her own practice, she had never had anything to lose by making a mistake. Now, things were entirely different.

"Fucking hell, I feel like some sort of conduit for evil." Catalina wrapped her arms around herself and shuddered.

"I suspect your statement is half right. You're a conduit—a powerful one. If the Council believed you were practicing dark magic, they'd have summoned you the first time someone fell ass over tea kettle into your memory." Brigitte shook her head as if she couldn't understand how the conversation had gotten so off track.

"Been there, done that on the ass over tea kettle thing." Tobi's giggle broke through the tension of the moment.

"I don't think you and Aunt Gigi are talking about the same thing, but I like your version better. Don't get me wrong, I love my grandfather, so my view of trips before the Magic Council is different, but let's face it… orgasms trump inquisitions."

"Good to know." Austin's voice sounded from the side

as he stalked from the shadows, pulling his wife to her feet to kiss her with enough heat to make the other women at the table swoon. Israel pulled Bristol to her feet as well and wrapped her in his arms.

I'm not happy with Brigitte. She should have given us a heads up about what she knew. I'm sorry I wasn't here when she hit you with both barrels. I believe Brigitte is honest, but her delivery could use some work.

Chapter Seventeen

ISRAEL WAS LIVID. Technically, Brigitte was in the right, but that didn't keep him from being frustrated with her. He hated knowing Bristol had been caught completely off guard in front of the women she considered her friends. He didn't have the impression she was close to the man and woman she knew as parents, but now, she'd be faced with grieving again... this time for her real family.

By the time the Wests picked up Tobi, Gracie, and Jen, he and Austin decided to table any discussion until they all had a good night's sleep. Israel ushered a very subdued Bristol to the elevator. The waves of confusion surrounding her were so dense, they were almost tangible.

"Tell me what you need, Bristol." Israel had his own opinion, but she needed to make the decision. Empowering his mate was the greatest gift he could give her, and he wasn't going to miss this chance to show her how serious he was about letting her set the pace.

"I'm not sure. I feel like I'm adrift in a raging sea, the engine won't start on the boat, and paddling would be an exercise in futility." That's where they disagreed. He thought a paddling might be just what she needed. Edging with pain before tipping over into pleasure might be just what the doctor needed. "I can't believe I'm saying this... but could you please give me what you think I need? Just take my mind off all this for a while?"

"It will be my pleasure, Beautiful." He meant every word. He intended to flood her with endorphins, giving her a physical reprieve and her brilliant mind a rest. Over the years, he'd known a lot of successful women who used BDSM as a way to escape their pressure-cooker lives—even if it was only for a night. They leapt at the chance to turn the decision over to a Dominant they trusted—a man or woman who could read their bodies like a book and meet every challenge.

Stepping into the cool suite, he noticed her shiver but knew it was more from anticipation than the chilled air. She hadn't had anything to drink for over an hour and reeling from the bombardment of information had burned off the last of the alcohol, but he planned to make certain she drank plenty of water before they started. Walking an emotional edge was usually a recipe for tears, and he didn't want there to be a risk of dehydration.

Handing her a bottle of water from the refrigerator, Israel nodded in approval when she started drinking. Stepping around her, Israel pulled a hair tie from his pocket and started finger-combing her hair. Once he'd divided it into sections, it didn't take him long to braid the long strands. She finished the water, and he turned her to face him.

"Strip." He didn't offer any explanation; this was about getting her out of her head. He'd use any means possible to help her forget the shit storm she'd stepped into—even for a few minutes. Brigitte was a closed book until she let him in. Her magical powers were phenomenal for her age. By the time she was her father's age, she would be a force, unlike any other.

Bristol pulled the sundress he'd given her earlier in the day over her head, leaving her standing nude.

"Fuck me, you are beautiful. I can't tell you how happy I am to see you are still bare beneath that dress." Glancing down to where the garment lay, he chuckled. "It's damned pretty, and it looks phenomenal on you, but after the day you've had, I'd understand if you wanted to toss it in the fireplace."

"It wasn't the dress' fault, and it was a gift from someone very important to me, so I think I'll save it."

Her words made his heart skip a beat—it was the first time she'd indicated there was more to their relationship than a few moments of pleasure, and he was important to her. *Progress*.

Leading her to the playroom, Israel wondered who was more nervous—Bristol because her anticipation and imagination were running rampant, or him because he wanted to exceed her expectations. Running his hands up her arms when she shivered, Israel was pleased to see goosebumps chasing his touch.

"What's your safe word, Bristol?" True to form, she repeated the spiel he knew had been driven into her during her training at the club. Repeating the words verbatim was easy for a sub—it was understanding when to say enough that usually presented a challenge. "If you'll let down your finely tuned defenses, I'll know exactly where you are every minute." He waited a few seconds for his words to move past the confusion of the day and imbed themselves in her soul.

Once he'd secured her to the St. Andrew's cross, Israel brushed the braid over her shoulder, letting his fingers linger, tracing the contours of the top of her shoulders before sliding slowly up the sides of her neck. Leaning forward, he spoke against the warm shell of her ear.

"I can hardly wait to claim you. Our blood mingling will send us both cartwheeling into an abyss where nothing matters but the connection between us and pleasure so deep, it's all-consuming. Everything will change for the better in a fraction of time so small, you'll barely know it's happened until a blinding burst of ecstasy flashes like lightning all the way to the deepest parts of your soul."

Moving back, he smiled when she pulled against the restraints, trying to maintain the physical connection. The key to making her his was not only ensuring the pleasure was too much to walk away from. Bristol had never known what it was to feel truly safe in another person's care. She'd been forced to raise herself. Her childhood was not only bleak, they'd recently learned it was all a lie.

Starting out slowly, he let her experience the feel of the leather strips of his flogger, sliding softly over the surface of her skin. He wanted her in the right headspace. It was important for her to let go in increments until they built enough trust for him to demand her to let go.

Warm. Sensuous. Tempting. How could I ever choose one word to describe the way it feels? He doesn't understand how much I want him, but everyone leaves. My heart would shatter if he left. I can't feel the loss if I don't let myself love.

Israel fought the urge to reassure her, letting her know how much she was revealing, but it was too early to show his hand. Moving the leather falls over her upper back, he watched pink bloom over her pale skin as the blood rushed to the surface. He wanted to give her body time to prepare itself for the more intense strikes he knew would send her into subspace, but she was fucking temptation personified. Her soft moans were going to be his undoing if he didn't concentrate.

"You're so responsive. It's a siren's call to a Dom, focused on their submissive's pleasure. I want to take you to levels of pleasure you have never dreamed existed. I'll hold nothing back from you." Upping the intensity of the strikes, Israel worked his magic over her shoulders and the center of her back before switching to the rounded globes of her ass. "I can smell your arousal, and it's making me crazy with the need to fuck you."

"Please. I want to feel you inside me. The burn of stretching tissue connects us. Your body pressed against mine grounds me. Words hot against my ear as you slide so deep, make me want to belong to you. Feeling the heat of your cock deep in my core is a dream come true."

As determined as he was to take it slow, her words broke his control. Israel tossed the flogger aside and hit the remote control he'd set on a nearby tray before shedding his clothes.

Bristol drew in a sharp breath when the platform she was standing on began to rise. The narrow ledge would raise her to the perfect height, so he'd be able to take her from behind without either of them worrying she'd slip from his grasp. The shift in position was enough distraction to allow her mind to reengage, moving her back from the edge. Pulling another flogger from the nearby cabinet,

Israel let her see the longer stands.

"Softer, but longer, this one is going to light you up, baby. Give the pain a chance to warm you, and the heat will push you right where you need to be." Her entire body stiffened with the first strike, the snap of stands wrapping around her hip to kiss the tender skin at the top of her mound. Letting his mind reach out to hers, Israel was thrilled when he heard her silently begging for more. Upping the intensity in small steps was important. A big push would register as too painful and make her safeword out. Small increases were interpreted by the body in an entirely different way, the increases in the pain moving her threshold higher and higher until the flood of endorphins sent her soaring.

BRISTOL WAS LOST in a maze of pain and pleasure, the sensations so close, she couldn't distinguish one from the other. Every strike sent her up a notch until she'd lost count, and her mind went blessedly blank. Letting go of all the heartache weighing her down hadn't been easy, but Israel was relentless. She could see why his flogging skills were something of a legend at Prairie Winds. When the platform started to rise, Bristol had been yanked back from the edge of the happy place, she wanted so desperately to visit.

The narrow ledge of the raised platform put her at the perfect height for Israel to take her from behind. She'd been anxious to feel him inside her but oddly disappointed when she felt her body moving away from the euphoria it had been chasing. Not fully cognizant, she'd been surprised how different the second flogger felt—the sting sharper, the heat left behind, searing. *Was it just a few seconds ago I regretted the loss of those wonderful neurotransmitters? Well, scratch that complaint. ASAP.*

Holy shit. Does anyone else hear a freight train? That was the last conscious thought she had before she felt herself floating. *Oh, yeah. Here. Right here.* Instinct took over as he slid deep inside her. Tilting her head to the side in a show of submission, Bristol bared her neck to him, a silent plea to be his. The move wasn't lost on Israel.

"Mine."

Her mind barely had time to process his snarled claim before the world around her exploded into dazzling white flashes of light. Heat burned like fire beneath where her shoulder sloped up to join her neck. The pain lasted no longer than a heartbeat before being chased away by the most profound pleasure she'd ever known.

Bristol's sex pulsed, the muscles of her vagina clench-ing so tight, she could feel Israel's pulse as blood pumped into his cock, his impressive size becoming longer and wider with every beat of his heart. As their blood mixed, Bristol saw flashes of his childhood flash through her mind. The brief glimpses reminded her of the old movies she'd seen, where you could tell the motion was made up of a series of still shots. His scent filled her nostrils, imprinting itself in every cell.

What seemed like long minutes could only have been a couple of seconds. It was startling how much could change in such a short time. The panic she'd expected to feel at surrendering her freedom was little more than a minor tightening in the center of her chest. Knowing she'd made such an enormous life decision in a moment of passion was totally unlike her, but as out of character as it was, she was oddly content with the result.

Israel's flogging skills proved to be everything the other subs raved about. Thinking about her mate's hands, touching another woman, made the hair on the back of Bristol's neck stand on end. She felt Israel slip from her with a rush of fluid, her face heating with embarrassment. He leaned back against her, his tongue caressing the two small puncture wounds she suspected were already healed.

"Don't get lost in things that are in the past, Bristol. No one can change their past. Worrying about it is a waste of your time and energy. From the moment I met you, no other woman held any physical appeal. You have a lot to learn about shifters. Mates are loyal to one another. There are many perks to being a shifter—enhanced senses, telepathic communication, and longer lifespans, and while I agree those are all important benefits, knowing we're mated for life and only have eyes for each other is what's most meaningful to me."

It took every ounce of her control to keep from bursting into tears. Bristol learned years ago how to bottle up her emotions, shoving them behind an invisible shield where they couldn't control her. As a physician, she had to make decisions based on facts rather than feelings. The habit was so deeply ingrained at this point, she felt blindsided by the emotions roiling through her.

"It's sub-drop, baby. Perfectly normal and something they should have covered in your training."

Israel's hands were hot on her shoulders, the heat of his

touch sinking bone-deep. Moving in measured increments down her arms, he finally reached her wrists and loosened the Velcro straps. Bristol gasped when the second restraint was removed, and her knees buckled. Israel caught her easily, pulling her back against his chest, holding her until she was steady on her feet. Bristol appreciated him giving her the opportunity to reserve a bit of dignity. Letting her walk from the room under her own steam made her appear stronger than she felt, and she was grateful.

"Beautiful, I had a wise father, a mother who didn't mind telling her sons exactly how they should treat women, and five sisters. Trust me when I tell you, they made certain the Adler brothers had a solid understanding of what it meant to be a mate." His amused tone made her smile, and she relaxed against him as they walked to the master suite.

Within a few minutes, he'd filled the massive bathtub with steaming water and poured in enough fragrant oil to make certain she lost herself in the scent of lavender and sage. Before she could sink into the water, Israel pinned her braid up. She smiled her thanks and let him help her into the water. Surprising her, he took a seat behind her, pulling her back between his splayed legs. Bristol gasped when his cock hardened against her lower back, astonished he seemed ready for round two so quickly.

"Baby, I'd have no trouble fucking you again this quickly, but your body needs rest."

He was right. She was exhausted—both physically and emotionally. Resting against Israel's chest, his legs bracketing her sides as his arms wrapped around her felt strange but perfect. Bristol couldn't remember a time when she'd been on such uneven ground emotionally.

"Is there a book?"

"Book? A book about shifters and mating?" Israel's chest vibrated against her back, and she wondered if he'd always be able to interpret her abbreviated questions.

Chapter Eighteen

"WRITTEN TOMES DO exist, but they aren't readily available." The truth was more complicated, but there wasn't any reason to rile up his little academic this close to bedtime. Hell, who was he kidding, a reasonable time to hit the sack passed hours ago.

"Isn't there some sort of shifter library, beginners' class, or something? How do youngsters learn everything? You keep mentioning things you learned as a child, but whoever raised me didn't bother to share any of these bits of wisdom. To be perfectly honest, I don't like being the odd one out when it comes to being informed. It's unfamiliar territory, and I… well, I hate it."

Lifting her, so he could turn her to sit on his lap, they weren't face to face, but it was better than talking to the back of her head.

"The books are kept in the Magic Council's library. They are heavily guarded and written in an ancient language only visible to a select few. Austin has been in the library. His stories are fascinating, and I'm sure he'd love to tell you about his experience."

"It's not some sort of secret, is it? I wouldn't want him to get in trouble for divulging classified information. Is there a Magic Bureau of Investigation? A Central Intelligence or MI6 group that polices this sort of thing? Holy crap balls, I was probably safer being completely ignorant. I don't do well with partial information. My mind won't let it go. Information is meant to be gathered. Facts analyzed. Ideas synthesized. Approaches amended." He was starting to worry about her passing out by the time she finally stopped to take a breath.

"The books are heavily guarded to keep them safe from nonmagicals. Those wishing to study in the library have to be sponsored by their Alpha. Many packs have complicated power structures. The two packs you'll deal with, do not. The Monroes share the Alpha position for their pack. I think you met my sister, London, at the wedding. She's married to both men. Aside from the Alpha title, their pack is run much like ours. The Alpha functions as a CEO and the pack is run much as any large corporation."

"Austin runs Adler Oil and the pack? How on earth did he find time to make a baby?"

"You'll find my brother is an excellent time manager. I'll admit, he was better when Charlotte was his executive assistant, but he's still phenomenal. He's also a ruthless delegator, so consider yourself forewarned." His comment brought a smile to her lips.

"Until I hired another physician, I rarely had any time off. Truthfully, I don't remember the last time I had a vacation. There wasn't really any reason to take one. Traveling alone never held any appeal for me, so I didn't bother scheduling time off."

Israel understood. He was accustomed to traveling alone for business, and it was damned lonely, and he'd never gone on vacation alone. When you grow up with nine siblings, you rarely go anywhere alone.

Lifting her in his arms, Israel stepped out of the tub and set his newly claimed mate on her feet. Wrapping a warm bath sheet around her, he was glad he'd pinned her hair up. She'd be in bed fast asleep in minutes. Patting her tender skin dry, Israel smeared a specially formulated moisturizer over her back and ass. The deep penetrating moisturizing cream was laced with an analgesic to neutralize any residual sting and help her sleep. Tucking her into his oversized bed, Israel shook his head at how young she looked.

He finished cleaning up the bathroom after a fast shower and was crawling in bed behind her within fifteen minutes. She was so sound asleep, her mind was completely silent. Maybe she'd learned to fall asleep quickly when the opportunity presented itself. He knew soldiers who swore combat taught them to sleep deeply when they could because the chances were often spaced far apart.

Wrapping his arms around Bristol and pulling her back against his chest, Israel smiled at her mumbled complaint about being moved. Smiling to himself, Israel breathed in her scent, noting the subtle differences since their mating. Another shifter would know immediately, she'd mated, and most would be able to identify who'd claimed her, but nonmagicals wouldn't be any wiser.

Before drifting off to sleep, Israel wondered if Bronx had any luck finding out who'd been breaking into his dealerships. Once Catalina found out there was an issue at the club and the women were meeting at Adler Oil, she'd come back to provide another layer of security, leaving Bronx on his own. Without conscious effort, Israel's mind briefly connected with his brother. Bronx was standing, hands on hips, speaking with a woman standing with her back to Israel. Petite and dressed in head-to-toe black, there was something vaguely familiar about her, but he cut the connection before he could be pulled into the scene. Israel would call Bronx tomorrow and find out how things went. He wasn't surrendering this moment with his mate. He'd waited too long for her to come into his life.

Mine!

"TELL ME YOU did not just bypass my security system and waltz into my dealership."

"Do you always have a stick up your ass?" Bronx ran his hand through his hair in frustration. Damn, this woman was a pain in the ass. "It's not my fault you haven't upgraded your system since Ronald Reagan was President."

"I was in fucking junior high." Good grief, what was her problem? She'd been spoiling for a fight since she pranced into his office ten minutes ago. "I admit the system needs to be upgraded, but it hasn't been a problem until recently."

"You're kidding yourself if you think this has been working. Hell, why don't you just pile empty tin cans under the windows every night? You could get one of those bells that hang over doors in charming little small-town diners… it would be as good as what you're using."

Damn, she was slick and had a smart mouth on her. It wasn't enough, this was the third facility she'd breached in as many hours? Now she was trash-talking him, too?

"Why is someone breaking in? Not one security camera gets a picture of the person's face. Instinct tells me it's a woman, based on the fluidity of the perp's movements, but that's a guess. Nothing is ever stolen. Whoever it is, accesses the system at this location with a small laptop, turns off the cameras for approximately twenty-eight minutes, then resets them. Just under the half-hour mark before alarms sound."

"Why half an hour?" He could practically hear the wheels of her quick mind spinning wildly as she tried to fit together all the pieces of the puzzle. Good luck with that. This train wreck had been making his life hell for months.

"Power outages for storms are usually less than half an hour. It was the lowest increment of time this system allows."

"Does this location have anything the others don't?" She snapped her fingers, and he saw her eyes light up. "Hot water showers?" Bronx felt things start falling into place. Hell, could it be that simple? She might be a smart mouth pain in his ass, but Brooklyn Adler was also one of the smartest women he knew. B, as the family called her, had spent years working for insurance companies, retrieving stolen artifacts and treasures from thieves. When Catalina bowed out of helping him tonight, he'd appreciated Brooklyn's offer to pinch-hit.

"Yes, and this facility is being accessed the most—actually three to four times a week."

"I'll have Luke send you some equipment that will work outside your existing system. No one should know about this but family." Bronx understood the underlying message, agreeing there was no reason to expose the burglar to more prying eyes than strictly necessary.

"I appreciate your help tonight, even if it doesn't seem like it. Something about this whole thing is off. It's just out of my grasp and driving me insane, trying to sort it out."

"You're welcome, and for what it's worth, I agree. You have to follow your gut. If this was a simple break-in, you'd have called the police the first time it happened. I think you're dealing with a woman; the residual energy is female." When he raised a brow in question, she shrugged. "I can feel her. She was here tonight. I think she left less than an hour before we got here."

"Why didn't I scent her? I've never been able to scent anyone other than staff when I've returned after hours."

"I don't know. She's probably masking it somehow. All I can tell you is the energy feels feminine, and..." It was unlike any of his sisters to hesitate in stating their opinion, making him wonder what was on Brooklyn's mind. She finally sighed, letting out a long breath. "There is a thread of hopelessness in the energy signature. I can't explain it, but it's there."

"She's right." They both gasped and turned to find Brooklyn's husband, Luke, standing a few feet away. "I left Crystal with Austin and Charlotte's nanny, so I could tag along, but I've been one step behind you all night. The two of you are a menace on the road."

"I can't believe you left our daughter with an unsuspecting nanny... that was just mean. She'll take over the place, rearrange furniture, change out the artwork. Damn, if Lindy quits, Charlotte is never going to forgive us, and I'm totally throwing you under the bus on this one."

Luke stepped forward, his posture changing from

loose-limbed casual to predator in a few steps. Bronx had never seen the sexual Dominant side of his brother-in-law—though he didn't doubt it existed—but it was on full display now.

"Our sweet little force of nature was fast asleep in Austin's arms when I left. She'd charmed him into sharing a huge bowl of ice cream covered in salted caramel. They'll both be in a sugar coma for hours—which is a good thing since my plans for the early morning have just changed." Brooklyn's cheeks were tinged with pink, the flare of heat in her eyes undeniable.

Cripes, get a damned room.

Turning to Bronx, Luke grinned. "I'll overnight the cameras and transmitters to you as soon as we get back to New Mexico. The pieces I want you to use won't be available locally."

Israel couldn't help but laugh. There was no doubt in his mind, the technology was military-grade. The products probably weren't commercially available anywhere yet.

Nope, nobody has these babies yet. They are hot off the press. Ian and I have been working on these for a while, and they are kick-ass.

Bronx laughed out loud.

"Damn, it's a good thing I'm used to dealing with Israel. That mind-reading crap might be a bit intimidating otherwise." As a shifter, Bronx was able to communicate telepathically when he was in his wolf, but as a human, it was much more challenging. Bronx could easily read people's emotions, gauge their desires, anticipate their reactions, but his most useful magical skill was being able to move through time. He was careful not to affect changes because the ripple effect was all too real. Whoever wrote the movie, *It's a Wonderful Life*, had known what they were talking about—even the smallest change could make an enormous difference that might be seen for generations.

Shaking his head in frustration, Bronx let his eyes move around the cavernous space. He'd worked many years to build up a business that, at this point, basically ran itself. The site managers at his dealerships were more than capable of functioning without him. Bronx hired competent people, trained them well, and treated them even better. His dad hadn't been the most successful businessman around, but he had known how to treat people—and taught his children to do the same.

Heaving an exhausted sigh, Bronx wondered if he should take the extended vacation he'd been considering. Spending a few months traveling sounded great, but something was holding him back. His photography hobby was fast becoming a booming business, but he wasn't entirely certain that was the direction he wanted to take it. When things started making money, were they still considered a hobby? He had plenty of money—what he needed was a creative outlet and someone to share his passion for photography.

What he needed was to solve the damn mystery of the break-ins. The hair stood up on the back of his neck as they walked to the door. Whoever she was, she was close—he could feel her, and it was damned spooky.

"Let it go. We'll figure it out." Luke's words were spoken quietly, the warning clear. *Don't search for her. Act normal.* Without missing a beat, Brooklyn chimed in, louder than her husband, her tone upbeat and non-threatening.

"It looks like a great car, but I'm not sold on the color. It's late, and I'm tired. I'm usually in bed long before now. Let's head back to the apartment. We have a long drive ahead of us tomorrow."

Bronx appreciated Brooklyn adding an air of informality when he'd felt every cell in his body go on alert. He'd never felt so tuned in to a person, he couldn't see and had never met. Was his mate lurking in the shadows? Why would she hide? And why break into his businesses? Nothing about the situation made sense.

Bronx couldn't wait to get the equipment Luke was going to send. If a woman was breaking in to use the shower, he wasn't thrilled about the Peeping Tom vibe, but it was only a matter of time before his staff starting noticing things were amiss. The site managers were sticklers for security and would call the authorities before Bronx would have a chance to intervene. Undermining their authority was off the table, so he needed to find out what was going on before things were out of his hands.

An hour later, Bronx gave up on sleeping and headed to the building's gym. He'd been living in one of the Adler Oil apartments after selling his home in Houston. Until he found something he liked in Austin, the two-bedroom suite was perfect. Stepping onto a treadmill, he smiled as Catalina joined him.

"Damn, Cat, you look as tough as I feel. What's up?" The slow jog he started with was embarrassing compared to the pace his sister set.

"Men. They're all a pain in the ass."

Okaaay, this conversation was off to a bangin' start.

"Since I'm sure you aren't talking about me, I'll take the bait. Problem in your love life, little sister?" When she glared at him, Bronx flashed her an unrepentant grin. "Won't work, baby girl. I'm immune to that look." Watching her in the mirror, Bronx didn't miss the flash of sadness in her expression. "Talk to me, sweetheart. I'm a good listener."

Bronx didn't know much about his sister's kidnapping, but he'd heard enough to know, she needed to work through the anger, or it was going to eat her up inside. He didn't push her—not that it would have done any good. Hell, none of his sisters could be pushed—they were the most stubborn women on the planet. They were also among the most loving and generous.

Catalina ramped up her speed to the point, he half expected the damned machine to start smoking or blow a fuse. Emotion was rolling off her in hot waves—anger, frustration, helplessness, fear—all powerful, but he knew his sister and knew it was the fear pissing her off. Since he hadn't seen Cooper Hicks at the wedding or since... Bronx assumed he was the man she was referring to, the question was—why and where was Hicks?

It was obvious Cat wasn't ready to talk, and he wasn't one to fill the silence with a bunch of idle chit chat. He slowly sped up his run, increasing the incline as well as he admired her speed and endurance. The woman was a fucking running machine. Drop-dead gorgeous, creative beyond measure, too smart for her own good and running on empty—not a good combination.

Chapter Nineteen

"**Y**OU CAN'T BE serious." Bristol was incredulous. What had she been thinking, mating with this Neanderthal? Where did he get off, telling her she couldn't go back to work until they managed to round up Nurse Nutsy? *What kind of high-handed, pig-headed, piss-off your ugly sister shit is this?*

"What did I say to make you think I was kidding?"

Israel could insert that faux calm directly up his perfect ass. His raised brow told her he'd heard her thoughts, but she didn't care. He'd just flipped her bitch switch. It was ordinarily well-guarded, but after the past few days, it had been right out there in plain sight.

"Perhaps you'd like to take a deep breath and calm down before we continue this discussion."

"Oh, brother, I cannot believe you just said that. I feel like a failure as a big sister. Hang on because you're about to get your ass handed to you."

Under different circumstances, Bristol would have found Asia's comments amusing, but she wasn't seeing the humor in anything at the moment. She was tired of being locked up like a damned prisoner when the crazy woman who'd bought a condo across from Israel's had been busy snapping pictures from across the street.

If you'd kept your fucking flogger to yourself, I wouldn't be in this damned mess. Tell me to calm down? I'll show you calm.

"Have you ever noticed, the person telling you to calm down is, without fail, the one who wired you up? Frosted Flakes, you are just too much, you know that? I don't know what I was thinking, mating with you. Let's kick off this discussion with the nonsense about me not going to the office tomorrow. I've already been off for several days. Good grief. Pregnant mamas don't give a fat rat's hairy ass about anything except getting their baby delivered safely— the sooner, the better. Babies don't care about what's going on outside their cozy living space until mama's tummy starts putting the squeeze on them, then they don't care who yanks them out."

"What the hell's going on? I could hear Bristol all the way down the hall?" Glaring at his brother, Austin fumed, "What did you do? Did you say something stupid?"

"He told her to calm down. Please tell me the security team isn't watching this, although I'd love to have a copy. I'm gathering clips for an Adler Siblings Dimmest Moments montage." Asia clearly had no interest in helping her brother, having decided his stupid remark had earned Bristol's wrath.

"Here's how it's going to be... I'm going to work. I have the panic alarm you gave me. I'll be fine." She rolled her eyes when they all looked surprised by her comment. "I swear, if I was as helpless as you seem to believe, I'd have never made it through my first year of medical school." Shaking her head, Bristol finally stopped pacing to face the three Adlers standing on the other side of the massive conference room table.

"Listen, I've agreed to meet London at the lab in my clinic in half an hour. She's going to draw the blood sample she needs for analysis and transport it back to her lab. They are flying out in an hour. Denali and Kensington are making an unscheduled stop in Boston tomorrow on their way to Paris for their honeymoon. If I don't do my part, Denali loses a chunk of her honeymoon for no reason, and I don't want to be responsible for that." Leaning across the table, her hands flat on the polished mahogany top, Bristol pulled in a steadying breath.

"I'm doing everything you've asked, except sitting on my thumbs. I have to work. Women depend on me. Their families count on me to keep their wives, mothers, sisters, and daughters safe through what is often one of the most stressful times of their lives. It's not fair to them for me to just disappear, and it isn't fair to ask me to walk away from my life's work because some floozy has her heart set on making you hers. She can kiss my ass. *You* are mine."

"Well played, Dr. B. Well played, indeed." Austin chuckled, but she could see admiration shining in his eyes. "Israel, she's your mate, and I won't presume to tell you how to handle this, but I will make a suggestion. One of your men was an Army medic, right?" Israel nodded but didn't take his eyes off Bristol. "Send him with her. She can pass him off as temp staff. It's not a perfect plan, but it buys you some time."

Bristol watched Israel's jaw tense, the shift so subtle, she'd have missed it if she hadn't been focused on his reaction to his brother's suggestion. It wasn't a perfect plan, but since she didn't have anything better and the clock was ticking, she'd take it.

It was amazing how fast people could get things done when they were motivated. A half-hour later, she escorted her new assistant into her clinic. She had to give Lincoln Billings credit, he'd hit the ground running. Bristol didn't know where he got them, but he changed into scrubs before meeting her in the parking garage, fifteen minutes after Israel's reluctant compromise.

London was the consummate professional, drawing several vials of blood and cautioning Dr. B to drink a lot of water and the bottle of juice she'd brought with her.

"I'm looking forward to this research. I haven't had anything new to work on for a while. This is a way for me to look out for my family from afar." Bristol detected a note of loneliness in the young scientist's tone but let it go when her husbands flanked her.

"Princess, you know we'll fly you to Texas anytime you want to visit your family." Eli's sweet words appeared to soothe London's anxiety.

"I can't always get away, Love, but Eli can usually work remotely." Dr. Evan Monroe was one of the country's best surgeons. Bristol understood his obligations better than anyone else could. He owned the surgical center, so the buck stopped with him.

Reaching out to London, Bristol grasped her forearm in what she intended to be a show of support. Gasping at the power surge she felt from the other woman, it took a few seconds for Bristol's brain to sort through the bombardment to her senses. Pulling London aside, Bristol made sure her back was to the Monroe brothers before giving the tiny blonde a warm smile.

"Congratulations, London. She's going to be gorgeous just like her mama." London's eyes filled with tears before she wrapped her arms around Bristol.

"Thank you so much. I haven't said anything to my mates, but I'm sure they know. They can always tell... well, they can tell everything. I think I could be across the country, and they'd call to tell me I'm ovulating and should get home right away. If they have their way, we'll have so many kids, I won't ever get any work done."

"I know you've been through this before, but every pregnancy is different. If you have any issues and can't get through to your doctor, please don't hesitate to call me." Bristol felt the Monroe brothers step up behind her and grimaced. Damn, she hadn't meant to spill the beans if they hadn't already figured out they were going to be fathers again.

"Come on, Princess. Evan has a patient being flown to Boston for surgery. Teenager with a compound fracture. Evidently, his dad is an ag pilot, and the two of them decided to see if they could snag the top wire of a fence. Obviously, it didn't work out well."

Watching the trio hurry out of the clinic, Bristol sent up a silent prayer for the young man headed to Evan's clinic and added one for the father who'd made a horrific decision. It wasn't a good sign he hadn't been mentioned.

Her new assistant stepped up beside her and held out his phone. "Don't worry about the dad. I Googled the accident; he walked away. He won't ever fly again, but all things considered, they're both damned lucky." She let out a relieved sigh and thanked him for the information. "The boss called. He was worried about you."

"What? Why?"

"Said something about you worrying about a patient. I explained what was going on. This is just a heads up; he is tuned in to you big-time." He blushed before adding, "I like this job, so if you could avoid getting me fired, I'd be most appreciative."

Bristol burst out laughing, unable to hold back her amusement. After everything she'd been through the past few days, getting a veteran fired was the last thing she wanted to do.

"Do you have any children?" she asked, looking at the ring on his left hand. When he shook his head, she grinned. "I'll make you a deal. You keep your boss' crazy stalker away from me, and I'll deliver your first baby for free." His face lit up as he laughed.

"Since my dad is a doctor in our small hometown, I know this is a huge gift." His smile faded, replaced by a sincere look of concern. "All kidding aside, I'll do whatever it takes to keep you safe, Doc."

How had she gone from feeling so alone a week ago to being surrounded by so many wonderful people a few days later? Proof you should never give up—everything could fall together as quickly as it fell apart. Patience and perseverance were the keys.

CLOVIA STOOD UNDER the awning, deep in the shadows, watching Dr. Bristol Banks run to the waiting car. The rain made it impossible for Clovia to identify the man following her, but he was obviously hired muscle—the scrubs he wore couldn't disguise his ultra-alert demeanor. He was a shifter with a medical background, she was guessing former military, probably employed by Israel Adler. He was easy on the eyes—it was unfortunate he had to die. Nobody was going to stand between Clovia and Israel Adler—not the hottie bodyguard or the bitch he was protecting. If Austin Adler didn't stop stirring up trouble in her pack, he was going on her damned hit list as well. Thank the Goddess, she'd anticipated his interference and made certain the calls to her Alpha were rerouted to a dummy phone. He'd catch on eventually... maybe. The man was so far up his wife's ass, it was a wonder Prairie Winds hadn't revoked his Dom card.

When she'd called the hospital today to let them know she was too ill to work, they'd politely informed her she was no longer needed. Clovia hadn't been surprised, but it still pissed her off. The Adlers were a powerful family of magicals. Making certain she no longer had a job would have taken little more than a phone call. It didn't matter, she had a very impressive trust fund, and the sale of her condo would fill her coffers even more. Of course, once Israel Adler was her mate, she wouldn't need to work. Dr. B was probably claiming she wasn't interested in the Adler fortune, but there wasn't an uncollared submissive at Prairie Winds who didn't want to be the one Master Israel claimed as his own.

Clovia was damned tired of pretending she wasn't a switch. Giving up opportunities to play the controlling role in D/s scenes had been a bigger sacrifice than she'd anticipated. Once Israel was hers, Clovia knew she'd be able to bend him to her will... at least occasionally. Until then, she'd continue playing the part of the devoted submissive. Cocking her head to the side, Clovia tried to identify the sound she'd heard. Muffled, she'd have never heard it without the enhanced senses of a shifter. She didn't have time to investigate. The car was already moving in her direction.

Pulling the gun from her pocket, Clovia raised it quickly, taking aim at the passenger in the approaching car. She squeezed the trigger, and everything around her exploded in a cacophony of deafening noise, bright lights, and total chaos—everything started to spiral downward. Her arm felt like it was set on fire. She screamed at the ferocious growl behind her before she was pulled to the ground, sharp teeth ripping the muscles of her upper thigh. The compelling voice of her Alpha cut through the blinding pain, his command to stop, coming a split second before she could shift.

Through the haze of pain, she saw Bristol Banks astonished expression framed by the undamaged window and illuminated by the streetlights as the car slowed briefly before speeding away. She didn't know why the shot hadn't taken the other women out, but there wasn't so much as a crack in the glass. Bound by the compelling magic of her pack's Alpha, Clovia remained frozen in place. Her mind screamed to shift, knowing how fast she would heal as a wolf, but the spell kept her locked in human form and drowning in agony. People were closing in around her, but she was so lost in pain, it was impossible to speak— hell, she could barely think.

AN HOUR AFTER Bristol left for her office that morning, Austin called Israel to tell him Clovia Williams' Alpha was on his way to Texas. Israel listened as his brother explained how he'd finally become suspicious about why his messages to the Alpha were being ignored. Deciding to use another contact, Austin got an immediate response. Before Bristol was finished seeing patients for the day, they had mobilized an operation that would have made the U.S. Joint Chiefs of Staff proud.

His mate only balked when she'd realized several people were putting their lives on the line to protect her. Israel was baffled. How could she expect anything less? In the end, it was Kent West who'd run interference. When he joined their heated video conference, Bristol had been in the middle of explaining, in excruciating detail, why Israel was an arrogant ass. Kent had burst out laughing before reminding Israel of all the times he'd laughed at Tobi's similar observations about her two husbands. Kent calmly explained this was business as usual for their team. In fact, they were deliberately overstaffing the operation to use it for training.

"Bristol, you know my brother and me well enough to have confidence in our ability to judge the potential danger in a situation. We'd never send our people in unless we knew they could handle any potential situation." He paused, letting her process his words before flashing her devious grin. "We're using this as a training exercise, Bristol. We damned well wouldn't send recruits into something we were overly concerned about. You put yourself in our hands when you joined the club, and we didn't let you down. Now, you're also under the watchful eyes of the entire Adler clan, as well as my lovely wife and her merry band of miscreants.

"Personally, if I was in Clovia Williams' position, I'd be more concerned with meeting the pissed off subs from Prairie Winds at a local social event. They are challenging on their best days, but they are all fiercely loyal. They understand the importance of friendship and function as a team when so many of their peers are competitive."

He paused for several seconds, studying Bristol's reaction, gauging her emotional state. He tilted his head to the side, a move Israel recognized as a prelude to a shift in the other man's approach. He listened as Kent laughed while shaking his head.

"Jen wanted me to make sure you know she's taking the second sniper position. She'll be on the roof of the building across the street from your clinic. I'll let her fill you in later on all the trash-talking taking place among our team. There seems to be a bit of competition about who will get to neutralize the threat to you. What I'm trying to say is, we've got your back. We'll only use the force necessary to keep you safe, but we will do whatever it takes."

Bristol had nodded solemnly and thanked Kent for taking the time to explain. Israel had been sitting on the edge of his chair during their conversation, watching his mate carefully, her face enlarged on the large screen on the wall, worrying about her lack of affect and the way her eyes glazed over. He wanted to go to her, offer his support, but she'd already been miffed when she left in the morning. London called him after drawing Bristol's blood, laughing about his mate's obvious frustration.

"Big brother, I'd like to tell you I feel sorry for you, but I don't."

He knew she was on her way to the airport, surrounded by her men. She might be able to fool most people with her teasing tone and cheerful demeanor, but he knew she'd been battling homesickness since she and her men arrived for Kensington and Denali's wedding.

"Don't be a stranger, sweetness. We miss you." She'd promised to return soon, but he made a mental note to check in with her soon. Something about the tone of her voice made him wonder what was up. Within minutes, he was up to his ass in alligators, making certain every detail of the day was mapped out, every contingency covered.

His security company had several fleet cars with bulletproof glass, but only one with armor plating in the side panels. Israel had been frustrated to hear the car was at one of Bronx's car dealerships for mechanical work. With Cleveland's racing background and Bronx's knowledge of every motor he'd ever sold, the two of them had worked all day to ensure the car was in perfect working order. Nobody wanted Bristol to be a sitting duck in a disabled car.

Five hours later, Israel stood deep in the shadows at one end of the block. He was grateful Kent and Kyle had been able to call in enough political favors to get a four-block square cordoned off for several hours. The official press release made a vague reference to a famous actor from Austin, filming a scene for an upcoming film. Since

Kensington Adler wasn't specifically mentioned, it didn't matter that he was enjoying a private flight bound for Logan International in Boston.

There weren't many places Kensington hadn't seen during his world travels, so the first place Denali mentioned, when he'd asked her where she would like to go on their honeymoon, was on the shortlist. They had planned to spend a couple of days exploring Salem, Massachusetts on their way home from Europe, but rearranged their itinerary when the Magic Council requested a blood sample from Denali.

Watching Bristol leave her clinic with another man at her side was a tough pill to swallow, but most of the team worried Clovia Williams wouldn't make a move if she saw him. His earbud was filled with chatter about locations and plans, but he'd tuned it all out the moment his mate emerged from her clinic. The first thing he noticed was her fatigue.

Bristol might not believe she needed a vacation, but everyone around her thought otherwise. Brigitte Stafford mentioned it to him earlier, promising to help Bristol find another physician to further lighten the load at her clinic. The Magic Council was pleased with the mini-baby boom taking place in central Texas but hadn't considered the strain it was putting on the local physicians specializing in the care of magical patients. The Council vowed to help, but their intervention wasn't going to come fast enough to eliminate the sag he could see in her posture.

Scenting Clovia hadn't been difficult. Her anger and the lingering stench from the horrible perfume she'd used while trashing Bristol's apartment gave away her location to every magical on the team. She wasn't expecting them, or she'd have covered the smell leaching from her pores. Fucking hell, that shit stunk to high heaven. Israel knew Bristol was safe inside the armored car, but watching Clovia raise the gun and fire at his mate made his heart skip several beats. Before he could suck in another breath, the sharp crack of a rifle bounced off the concrete and steel buildings lining the street. The gun flew from Clovia's hand, clattering to the ground in front of her as she grasped her upper arm, howling in pain. The wolf that emerged from the black smoke filling the air behind Clovia, lunged, latching on to the woman's upper thigh, the bite meant to keep the nurse in place.

The wolf disappeared as quickly as it appeared, and in its place was a stern-looking man, standing next to Brigitte Stafford. Hell, now he wasn't sure which one of them had shifted in the cloud of black smoke, but his money was on Brigitte since she was perfectly clothed rather than stark naked the way most shifters would be. Laughing to himself, Israel moved quickly down the street, stepping up to a semi-circle of men and women in time to hear Kent West whistle.

"Holy fucking hell. Remind me to never piss one of you off. Shit."

Sam McCall looked up and laughed. "Guess we don't have to check the ballistics to see who fired the shoulder shot." Sam and Sage's wife, Jen, was standing next to a disgruntled looking Sage. Excitement vibrated from her, the waves so strong Israel could feel them all the way down on the sidewalk. Jen fist-pumped the cool, night air, and blew kisses down to Sam while Sage tried in vain to pull her back from the roof's edge.

Police Chief Parker Andrews shook his head. "I'm glad we cordoned off the area, or I'd be answering calls from every media outlet in the damned free world. Hell, I'm not even sure what I'd tell them."

"The Council and her pack are claiming first dibs, Parker. You okay with that?" Austin gave his friend and fellow Dom a considering look. Israel knew Parker had been briefed about the expectations of the growing magical community in Austin, so big brother's question was merely a formality.

"Off the record? Yes. I'm sure their justice system works much faster than ours. I don't expect to see her back on the street in two hours, and that's a virtual certainty if I take her in."

"I don't want to think about the volume of paperwork involved with this case—a shot fired at a popular local physician, in an area cordoned off for a movie scene no studio would know anything about, and security feeds scrambling a four-block section of the city. Hell, you'd be buried alive by the paperwork before the media ever got their chance." Kyle West slapped Parker on the back before turning to Israel.

"Go. I'm sure Bristol is rattled. It's damned scary having someone point a gun at you and pull the trigger—I don't care if you are in a fucking tank." Israel agreed, and he'd seen the bullet bounce off the glass. Clovia Williams had wanted to put a bullet right between Bristol's eyes. The woman was fucking nuts. "We're going back to the armory. I want to help debrief our trainees and remind them about the NDAs they signed."

"I bet some of them are having Will Smith moments from Men in Black... that 'I can't fucking believe what I just saw' realization. Finding out there is more to the world than you'd ever dared to imagine is eye-opening." Israel knew the Chief of Police experienced those same eye-opening moments a couple of years earlier, an experience Parker told Israel and Austin had changed his world view between one breath and the next.

"Since we don't have one of those fancy flashy things that will wipe out recent memory, we need to be there before the trainees disperse. It won't take them long to clean and store their weapons since Jen is the only one who got off a shot."

"Something we'll be hearing about for years to come." Kyle chuckled, shaking his head as he looked at Sam McCall.

"Don't look at me. You knew better than to give those two the best sniper seat in the house. Although I have to admit, I'm anxious to see what our lovely sub promised my brother in exchange for taking the first shot. I fully intend to reap the benefits."

Israel knew the McCalls played good cop bad cop with their sub, very much like the Wests. Both women were spirited enough, it took two Doms to keep them in line. Israel laughed about how liberally he was applying the term, *in line*.

As the group broke up, Israel turned to walk back to the parking garage, nearly tripping over Brigitte. "Damn. Sorry, I didn't realize you were behind me." He grasped her shoulders to keep from knocking her to the ground, gasping at the sizzle of power he felt vibrating beneath his touch.

"I just got here—I was dealing with Ms. Williams. She is in the custody of the Magic Council. Please reassure Dr. Banks, the other woman is receiving the medical care she needs, then she will be in custody for the foreseeable future. If reprogramming isn't successful, she'll be stripped of all special abilities and will remain confined."

Israel nodded and waited. The power of her magic blocked his empathic skills, but Brigitte's expressions made her an open book when she was dealing with friends and family.

"If the blood tests come back the way we suspect they will, we'll be able to introduce Bristol to family members who have been looking for her for a long time. Denali already has some family history knowledge, thanks to her grandfather. Her clear ties to both the Eskimo and Native American cultures go a long way to explaining why she's a conduit for magic. Both women have vast reserves of magic—far more than they know. The Council of Magic will help them tap into and channel it. We want to keep them off the dark force's radar as long as we can."

"Keep us posted. In the meantime, I'm going to keep her as close as possible." He smiled down at Brigitte before pulling her into a quick hug. "Take care, Brigitte. Thanks for your help and for bringing the issue of increased medical care for our community to the attention of the powers that be. Their help will be greatly appreciated." Even in the dim light, he could see her cheeks tinge pink. Humble looked awfully sweet on the woman whose witchcraft was the envy of every magical he knew.

"I'll be in touch. Invite me to the wedding. Be nice to

my nephew." Three short sentences and she was gone. No flashy wave of the cape, no mystical smoke—just gone. It was as disconcerting as it was impressive.

Chapter Twenty

Two months later

K ODI WEST BOUNCED up to the picnic table, setting her plate between her two grandfathers, and flashed them a grin, Israel suspected the little imp learned from Lilly. He'd also bet his sizeable savings, her radiant smile rarely failed to get her whatever she wanted from the two older men.

Del looked at her and chuckled. "Damn, girl, you look just like those hippy chicks we saw in California when we were young bucks."

"Dad, I doubt she is familiar with the hippy counter-culture movement."

"Sure, I am familiar with all the cool things that happened during the sixties. Gramma told me all about it. If you were a hippy, you got to dress funky, wear flowers in your hair, and travel without leaving home."

Kent West snorted tea from his nose, and Kyle looked like he'd swallowed a lemon. Kodi's studious twin, Kam, sat down next to Kent and rolled his eyes.

"She used some nasty citrus stuff on her hair last summer, trying to get it to streak when she was in the pool. I swear she bleached out her brain cells instead."

"You can kiss my perky derriere, Sherman."

Kam rolled his eyes again and shook his head, obviously accustomed to his sister's taunts.

"Dad, you *really* need to cut off the cable in her room. She watches all the oldie cartoons, and it's turning her brain to mush." It was impossible to miss the disdain in Kameron West's young voice. The kid was the spitting image of his dads, but his attitude was all Kyle. Kam had yet to learn discretion, but the kid was surrounded by mentors, not only his fathers and grandfathers, but their friends and associates as well. Israel doubted Kam's mother or grandmother would let him go too far over the line with his sister before clipping his wings.

Del looked at his grandson and shook his head. "She's gonna kick your ass, you know. You keep thinking you're all that and a bag of chips, you'll never find a girlfriend."

"You're the best, Papa Del." Kodi leaned into her grandfather, giving him a tight hug and kissing his weathered cheek. "I can always count on you and Papa Dean to have my back. Kam thinks he's smarter than I am because he gets better grades, but he has no life. He studies all the time. When we go to college, I'm going to acclimate so much faster than Sherman will, you watch and see."

"Wasn't Mr. Peabody the super smart one and Sherman, his adopted son/student?" Israel remembered the cartoon. Hell, it had been old when he was a kid—if Kodi was watching it, she was probably doing so on YouTube.

"Yes, but I'm not calling Kam Mr. anything. Nope, not happening."

"You won't get the chance to call me anything. I'm

going to invent a time machine to launch your happy self back to the sixties. You'll be able to hang out with the creators of The Flintstones, Mr. Magoo, Top Kat, and all the other goof troop nonsense you're using to shave points off your IQ at an alarming rate."

Kyle looked at Israel and rolled his eyes. "Your parents must have been promoted to saints the minute they hit the other side. These two are going to drive me to drink. I can't imagine what it was like with ten kids under one roof."

Israel laughed without bothering to mention there were times he missed the chaos so much, he felt it to the depths of his soul. A wave of sadness threatened to swamp him until warm hands softly massaged the tops of his shoulders. Every ounce of the tension he'd felt instantly drained from the muscles as his mate pressed her softness against his back.

"SORRY I'M LATE. I tried to tell the babies I delivered this afternoon that I had an *important* party to attend, and it was okay to ignore the full moon, but they weren't having it."

"Bet their mamas weren't interested in waiting either." Tobi West's tinkling laughter made her husbands smile as she settled on Kent's lap.

"Geez, Mom, must you be so…" Israel heard the rest of Kodi's unspoken statement and wondered for a second if it was something she'd expressed before when her fathers frowned.

"Be *very* careful, Kodi. We won't tolerate disrespect,

particularly when it is directed at your mother. Your tone speaks as clearly as your words." Kyle's reprimand hit the mark. The sassy young girl nodded without saying any more. Tobi looked over his shoulder at Bristol and grinned.

"Have you eaten? There's still a ton of food inside. It would be a shame for you to go hungry when you and Israel are the guests of honor." Without waiting for Bristol to answer, Tobi scrambled to her feet, the petite, blonde dynamo motioning her friend to follow. "Come on. I wanted to talk to you, anyway. No reason to trouble our men with girl talk."

Israel felt the hair on the back of his neck stand on end. Anytime Tobi avoided speaking in front of her Doms, trouble was brewing. Judging by their matching furrowed brows, Kent and Kyle experienced the same sense of foreboding.

"Damn and double damn." Tobi laughed as they made their way inside. "Israel looked like he wanted to pry you out of my wicked clutches. I swear everyone thinks I'm a troublemaker—it's positively insulting."

"And well earned." Jen stepped around the corner and laughed at Tobi's frown before turning her attention to Bristol. "Hey, girlfriend, long time no see." Giving her a quick hug, she looked over her shoulder and nodded to someone Bristol couldn't see before silently mouthing the words, *not my fault.*

"Jen, I can't believe you are wimping out. Dr. B didn't get to have a proper bridal shower before eloping, and we didn't want her to miss the joy of being properly embarrassed by her friends."

Jen McCall leaned close to whisper, "Don't worry, it's

just a naughty teddy shower."

Bristol nodded numbly, not entirely sure what a teddy shower involved. At the moment, she was too focused on the huge number of women filling the main room of the Prairie Winds Club. Equipment had been moved against the walls and partially hidden by colored screens, and there were rows and rows of chairs, all filled with chattering women, who stood to applaud when they saw her standing at the door.

Denali's beaming face smiled down at her from a large screen, waves slapping against a white sand beach in the background. Bristol gave her a shy wave, remembering Kensington was working on a movie somewhere in the Caribbean. London and Paris smiled and waved from a second large screen before London suddenly covered her mouth and darted out of sight. Evidently, the other woman's tender tummy still hadn't adjusted to its newest resident.

Paris shrugged. "Guess it's just going to be me until the little Martian stops turning her mama green."

Everyone laughed before their attention turned to the woman with the pink hair... no wait, now it was red. Slender legs clad in skintight jeans and black leather boots with sky-high heels ate up the distance between them, her long strides closing in fast. The flowing blouse Brigitte wore billowed softly behind her, leaving a trail of brightly colored glitter, the wild print reminiscent of the pictures Bristol had seen of the flower children of the 1960s.

"Congratulations, Bristol. The members of the Magic Council send their best wishes as well. They are looking forward to meeting with you next week. They should have the test results by then." Brigitte nodded to Asia and Catalina, who'd stepped up on Bristol's left, before hugging her niece, Charlotte, who'd appeared on Bristol's left.

"Now, since I wasn't invited to the elopement, I'm looking forward to this event." The powerful young witch looked around and grinned, "You have an impressive number of friends, Bristol. Let's see what naughty bits they brought."

The End

Books by Avery Gale

The Adlers
Brooklyn
London
Austin
Paris
Cleveland
Asia
Kensington
Israel

The ShadowDance Club
Katarina's Return – Book One
Jenna's Submission – Book Two
Rissa's Recovery – Book Three
Trace & Tori – Book Four
Reborn as Bree – Book Five
Red Clouds Dancing – Book Six
Perfect Picture – Book Seven

Club Isola
Capturing Callie – Book One
Healing Holly – Book Two
Claiming Abby – Book Three

Masters of the Prairie Winds Club
Out of the Storm
Saving Grace
Jen's Journey
Bound Treasure

Punishing for Pleasure
Accidental Trifecta
Missionary Position
Another Second Chance
Star-Crossed Miracles
Dusted Star
Lilly's Choice

The Wolf Pack Series
Mated – Book One
Fated Magic – Book Two
Tempted by Darkness – Book Three

The Knights of the Boardroom
Book One
Book Two
Book Three

The Morgan Brothers of Montana
Coral Hearts – Book One
Dancing with Deception – Book Two
Caged Songbird – Book Three
Game On – Book Four
Well Bred – Book Five

Mountain Mastery
Well Written
Savannah's Sentinel
Sheltering Reagan

The Christmas Painting
Taking Out the Mother of the Bride

I would love to hear from you!

Email:
avery.gale@ymail.com

Website:
www.averygale.com

Facebook:
facebook.com/avery.gale.3

Twitter:
@avery_gale